Cy Warman

Tales of an Engineer with Rhymes of the Rail

Cy Warman

Tales of an Engineer with Rhymes of the Rail

ISBN/EAN: 9783337274252

Printed in Europe, USA, Canada, Australia, Japan

Cover: Foto ©Andreas Hilbeck / pixelio.de

More available books at **www.hansebooks.com**

TALES OF AN ENGINEER

WITH

RHYMES OF THE RAIL

TALES OF AN ENGINEER

WITH

Rhymes of the Rail

BY

CY WARMAN

NEW YORK

CHARLES SCRIBNER'S SONS

1896

₊ *These tales are republished, by permission, from McClure's Magazine, the Engineering Magazine, and the Youth's Companion. The rhymes are mostly from the New York Sun.*

𝔘𝔫𝔦𝔳𝔢𝔯𝔰𝔦𝔱𝔶 𝔓𝔯𝔢𝔰𝔰:

JOHN WILSON AND SON, CAMBRIDGE, U.S.A.

TO THE GREAT ARMY OF

Enginemen,

THE SILENT HEROES WHO STAND ALONE AND
BORE HOLES IN THE NIGHT AT THE
RATE OF A MILE A MINUTE,

THESE TALES ARE DEDICATED.

THE AUTHOR.

CONTENTS

GOD, WHO MADE THE MAN.

I hear the whistle sounding,
　　The moving air I feel;
The train goes by me, bounding
　　O'er throbbing threads of steel.

My mind it doth bewilder
　　These wondrous things to scan;
Awed, not by man, the builder,
　　But God, who made the man.

A Thousand-Mile Ride on the Engine of a "Flyer"

I

A THOUSAND–MILE RIDE ON THE ENGINE OF A "FLYER"

A THOUSAND miles in a night — in one sleep, as the Indians say — was what I wanted to do ; and I wanted to do it on a locomotive. I searched some days in vain for an opportunity. Then I was introduced to Mr. H. Walter Webb, third Vice-President of the New York Central Railroad, told him my trouble, and promptly received permission to ride the engine that pulled the "Exposition Flyer." The artist who was to accompany me as promptly received permission to occupy the attending train.

When, on the afternoon of September the 26th, I went down to take my run out, one hundred and one passengers were waiting in the Grand Central Station with tickets for

Chicago by the "Flyer." It was 2.45, fifteen minutes before leaving time. At 2.55 they were all aboard. A little ahead of my turn, I showed the gate-keeper an order signed by the Superintendent of Motive Power, which gave the engineer authority to carry me on the locomotive, and passed to the train. I found a little wiry engineer standing right in under the boiler of the 898, oiling her link motion.

A one-hundred-pound engineer and a one-hundred-ton locomotive! A little bird chasing an eagle across the sky! Each seemed to exaggerate the other. How different was this mammoth machine from the mountain climbers I had been used to — built so near the ground that to get under them the engineer must lie flat down and crawl.

As the great clock in the despatcher's office pointed to 2.55 the driver began to glance at his watch. Then he climbed up into the cab, exchanged oil cans, climbed down, and walked around the locomotive, dropping a little oil here and there — giving her a last finishing touch. Then he put his foot first against the main, then the parallel rods, to see if they moved easily on the pins. Already I had introduced myself to the engineer, and was now on the engine making friends with the fireman. At 2.59 we were all in the cab. The pointer stood at one hundred and eighty pounds; the fireman leaned out of the window just behind me, looking toward the rear of the train. Glancing over at the engineer, I noticed that he was looking ahead, and that his left hand was on the throttle. Just as I looked back, the conductor threw up his right hand, the fireman shouted "All right," the throttle flew open, and the first great exhaust seemed to lift the roof from the shed. The drivers are so large — six feet six — that with each exhaust the train moves forward nearly five feet, and with each revolution we are nineteen and one-half feet nearer our journey's end.

Whatever of anxiety I might have felt an hour ago is gone; and as the proud machine sweeps over switches, through tunnels, under bridges, and through suburban New York, and finally around to the shores of the Hudson, all thought of danger has vanished, and I know that I shall enjoy the ride. Nearly a thousand miles of rails reach out before us, but to me the way seems short.   I hear the click of the latch as the engineer cuts the reverse-lever back, shortening the valve stroke and increasing the speed.   As often as he does this he opens the throttle a little wider, until the pressure in the steam-chest is almost equal to the pressure in the boiler.   Every time he touches the throttle the swift steed shoots forward as a smart roadster responds to the touch of the whip.   When the lever is forward and the stroke is long, the steam flows in at one end of the cylinder, and pushes the piston head to the other end.   When this exhausts, another flow of steam enters the other end of the cylinder to push the piston back.   The result of this is a continuous flow of steam through the valves, and a useless waste of water and fuel.   When the stroke is short, the valve moves quickly.   With an open throttle the steam darts from the steam-chest, where the pressure is high, to the cylinder; another quick movement of the valve closes the port, and the expanding steam does the rest.

The long, heavy stroke is necessary only in starting trains and on heavy grades.

Absence, we are told, makes the heart grow fonder. The pain of parting is all forgotten in the joy of meeting; and now as we begin to swing round the smooth curves, all the old-time love for the locomotive comes back to me. The world will never know how dear to the engineer is the engine. Julian Ralph says, "A woman, a deer, and a locomotive." The engineer would say, "A woman, a locomotive, and a deer."

Again I hear the click of the latch, and a glance at the ground tells me that we are making forty miles an hour. The scene is impressive. The many threads of steel stretching away in the twilight; the river on one side, on the other a rock wall, and above the wall the vines and trees; the gentle hills beyond the Hudson where the leaves are turning with the touch of time — the end of summer at the death of day !

Now the people along the line begin to look for us : every one seems to expect us, except two Italian women who are walking near the wall. They hear the whistle, look back, and see the great engine bearing down upon them at a fearful rate. I glance at the engineer, whose grim face wears a frown, and whose left hand moves nervously to the air valve, then back to the throttle.

Panic-stricken, the women start to run, but in a moment we dash by them. The wind of the train twists their clothes about them, pulls their bonnets off, while their frightened faces are whipped by their loosened hair. A step on one of the sleepers strikes the basket on the arm of one of the women, and a stream of red apples rolls along the gutter, drawn by the draught of the train. Now the smoke clears from the stack, the engine begins to swing and sway as the speed increases to forty-five or fifty miles an hour. Here and there an east-bound train brushes by us, and now the local which left New York ten minutes ahead of us is forced to take our smoke. The men in the signal towers, which succeed one another at every mile of the road, look for the " Flyer," and each, I fancy, breathes easier when he has seen the swift train sweep by beneath him.

Everything appears to exaggerate our speed, which is now nearly a mile a minute. An ox-team toiling up a little hill serves to show how fast we go. As we sweep by a long freight train, west-bound, it is hard to tell whether it is running or standing still. In fact, we cannot tell until we come up to the locomotive and hear one loud exhaust, and we are gone.

When the whistle sounds, the fireman looks ahead, and if the signals are right, he shouts to the engineer. If the road is curving to the left, it is not always easy for the engineer to see the signal displayed. The fireman even tries the water. Fifteen years ago that would have cost him his job. "You keep her hot; I'll keep her cool," the engineer would have said at that time. And yet he should be glad to have some one help him watch the water, for nothing brings such lasting scandal to a runner as the burning of an engine. He may run by his orders, but if he drops his crown sheet he is disgraced for life.

We are now fifty minutes out; the throttle is closed. A half mile ahead is the water trough. When the engine reaches it, the fireman drops a spout, and in thirty seconds the big track trough is dry. When the tank is filled the throttle is opened, the fireman returns to his place at the furnace door, and in a few minutes we are sailing along the line as fast as before. The black smoke curling gracefully above the splendid train reminds me of what Meredith said of his sweetheart : —

> " Her flowing tresses blown behind,
> Her shoulders in the merry wind."

We have lost a minute or a minute and a half taking water, and now we are nearing a bad bridge — a bridge under repair, and over which the engineer has been instructed, by a bulletin posted in the round house at New York, to pass at ten miles an hour. We are three minutes late, when again we get them swinging round the curves beyond the bridge ; for it must be remembered that the Central's track along the Hudson is far from straight, though the road bed is so nearly perfect that passengers in the coaches do not feel the curves. Every one seems to know that we are three minutes late. The old man with the long-handled wrench, tightening up the bolts in the rails, reproaches the engineer with a sort of " What 's-de-matter-wid-yez?" expression, as we pass by.

The man in the next tower is uneasy till we are gone.

We are a hundred miles from New York now, and although I carry a time-card, I am unable to read the names on the stations. Holding my watch in my left hand, I tap the case with my right; the engineer shakes his head slowly, and holds up three fingers: we are three minutes late. I cross over, take a seat behind the driver, and, speaking loud at the back of his neck, express the hope that we shall reach Albany on time.

He says nothing. I cross back to the other side, and as often as he whistles I ring the bell. A minute later he turns to the fireman and shouts: "Look out for her, Jack," at the same time pulling the throttle wide open. Jack knew his business and proceeded to look out for her. Taking the clinker hook, he levelled off the fire, shook the grates, and closed the furnace door. The black smoke rolled thick and fast from her stack, then cleared away, showing that she was cutting her fire beautifully. Swinging the door open, the skilled fireman threw in three or four shovels of coal, closed it, and leaned out of the window, watching the stack. The trained fireman can tell by the color of the smoke how the fire burns.

The few pounds of steam lost in fixing the fire, and by reason of the throttle being thrown wide open, are soon regained. The pointer goes round to 190, and the white steam begins to flutter from the relief valve at the top of the dome. She must be cooled a little now, or she will pop, and waste her energy. An extra flow of cold water quenches her burning thirst, and she quiets down. How like a woman when her heart is hurt! She must be soothed and petted, or she will burst into tears and sob herself away.

Now we turn into a long tangent, and are clipping off a mile a minute. Our iron steed trembles, shakes, and vibrates a little, but aside from the fact that there is some dust, the cab is not an uncomfortable place. The exhausts, that began in the Grand Central station like the explosion of a shotgun, come so fast, so close together, that they sound like the drumming of a pheasant's wings.

The sun sinks behind the big blue mountains,

the shadows creep across the valley, and up to our window comes the faint perfume of the fields—the last scent of summer in the soft September winds. Here and there we can see the lamps lighted· in the happy homes by the Hudson, while the many colored signal-lamps light up our way.

Not long ago I stood for the first time on the deck of a steamer bounding over the billowy bar at the mouth of the Columbia River, and was filled with a reckless joy. Looking down at the little woman who hung to the railing near me, I beheld a face radiant with rapture. "How is it?" I asked. "It's worth drowning for," was her answer; and so I reckon now. Taking into consideration all the risk, and the fact that I must remain on this narrow seat for twenty hours, yet I am forced to confess that so grand a trip is but poorly paid for.

If I am at all uneasy it is only when turning the slightly reversed curves where the way changes from a two to a four track road, or back. Plain curves are all well enough. But it does not seem quite right to shoot her into those kinks at a mile a minute. Yet after I have seen her take two or three of these, I rather enjoy it. She sways to the right, to the left; then, with a smart shake of her head when she finds the tangent, she speeds away like the wind.

Every man in the employ of a great rail-road company plays an important part. These smooth curves, perfectly pitched, are the work of an expert trackman. The outer rail must be elevated according to the curve, and with full knowledge of the speed of the trains that are to use the track. I have seen a train on a heavy grade, drawn by two strong locomotives, when nearly stalled on a sharp curve, lift a sleeper from the middle of the train and turn it over. It was because the curve was too sharp, and the elevation too great, for so slow a train.

The engineer looks across the cab and smiles, and I know that he has taken my hint about reaching Albany on time good-naturedly; we understand each other. In his smile he asks: "How do you like it?" and I answer by raising my right hand with all save the first finger partly closed, and with a slight turn of the wrist give him that signal so well known to train and engine men, which means "All right; let her go."

We were due at Albany at 5.45, and at 5.40 the fireman stepped over and shouted in my ear: "That big building at the end of the stretch there is the capitol of the State;" and the "Exposition Flyer" rolled into Albany on time.

An extra sleeper, well filled with the good people of the capital, was switched to our train. Saying good-by to the old crew, I swung into the cab of the 907. The engineer shook hands warmly, said he expected me, introduced me to his fireman, showed me a comfortable seat directly behind him, and opened the throttle. This locomotive was nearly new, black and beautiful.

I noticed that we pulled out a few minutes late. There is a heavy grade out of Albany, and though we had a helper pushing us over the hill, it seemed as if we should never get them going; and when we did, we were six minutes behind our card time. The fireman, with whom I sympathized, worked hard, but he was handicapped. The hard pounding up the hill had torn holes in his fire. His furnace door worked badly — it would not stay open; and to make a misstroke with a single shovel of coal on such a train is not without its bad effect. The gauge lamp bothered him. Twice he had to climb to the top of the big boiler and re-light it. The additional car, too, told on the locomotive, and it seemed impossible, though the crew worked faithfully, to get a mile a minute out of her. When the engineer shut off to slow for a station, running without steam, she swept over the steel track as smoothly as a woman rides on roller skates, making little more noise than a coach. She was the smoothest rider and the poorest " steamer " of the lot; but it does not follow that with all things working well she would not steam, nor was her crew at fault. But so important are the moments on a train like this, that the least mishap is as fatal as for a trotting-horse to slip in the start.

A number of little things, including a bad stop at a water-spout, put us into Syracuse six minutes late; and the gentle and gentlemanly engineer, for whom I was really sorry, showed plainly his embarrassment.

A jolly-looking young man was the engineer of the 896. This crew was a little remote, I thought, at first. But when they had seen my credentials they thawed out; and although we left eleven minutes late, the ride to Buffalo was a delightful one. Just as we were pulling out, one of the black boys from the "diner" came to the engine with a splendid luncheon, sent over by Conductor Rockwell. We were soon going. Holding the plate on my lap, I began to devour the eatables; but as the train began to roll about, I was obliged to throw the luncheon out of the window, almost losing the plate as I did so. But I held to a half-gallon pail which was nearly full of steaming coffee. I asked my friends to join me, but they shook their heads. The engine rolled more and more, as did the coffee; and the boys laughed as I stood tiptoe, taking one long drink after another. I passed the pail to the fireman, who was about to dash it away; but, catching scent of the coffee, paused, and passed the pail up to the engineer, who took a good drink. The fireman then took a good drink too, and would have emptied the pail; but I touched him on the shoulder, and he passed it to me. I took another drink, all hands smiled, and we settled down to business.

I had been riding on the fireman's side for half an hour when the jolly driver motioned me over, and I took a seat behind him. This locomotive was not very new, but she was a splendid "steamer." The fireman appeared to play with her all the while. The track was straighter here, but not so good. This made no difference with the bold young man at the throttle.

"How old are you?" said I.

"Twenty-five."

"How long have you been running?"

"Twenty-two years," he said.

I don't know whether he smiled or not, for I saw only the back of his head. These men on the "Flyer" seldom take their eyes from the rail. I expressed anew a wish that we might be able to make up the lost time.

"I think we shall," he said, and he pulled the throttle lever back toward the tank.

It was nearly midnight now, and the frost on the rail caused the swift steed to slip. When

we had reached the speed of a mile a minute,
and gone from that to sixty-five miles an hour,
I thought she would surely be satisfied; but
every few minutes her feet flew from under her,
and the wheels revolved at a rate that would
carry her through the air a hundred miles an
hour. The engineer stood up now, with one
hand on the throttle, the other on the sand
lever; for it is not quite safe to allow these
powerful engines to slip and revolve at such a
rate.

"We 've got twenty-eight miles up-hill now,"
said the engineer, as he unlatched the lever
and gave her another notch. The only effect
was a louder exhaust, and a greater strain on
the machinery. It seemed the harder he hit
her, the better she steamed; and we went up
the hill at almost a fifty-mile gait.

"Now it is down hill to Buffalo," said the
driver; and, as the speed increased to sixty-
five, seventy, and then seventy-five miles an
hour, the sensation was delightful.

"We 've got thirty-six miles now, and thirty
minutes to make it in," said the man at the
throttle.

"And you 've got your nerve also," said I in a whisper. Orchards, fields, and farms sweep by, and the very earth seems to tremble beneath our feet. The engine fairly lifts herself from the rail, and seems to fly through space.

We stopped at Buffalo at 11.39, just one minute ahead of time, and this remarkable run was made over the poorest piece of track on the main line of the New York Central and Hudson River Railroad. Eight hours and forty minutes, and we are four hundred and forty-four miles from New York.

The men who manned the 898 and the 907 are sound asleep, and this last crew will be so within an hour. The flagman and brakeman meet for the first time since they left New York, come forward to ask how I like it, then drift into the station, "jolly up" the girl at the lunch counter, pay for their luncheon, "stand" her "off" for a couple of cigars, and go out into the night. These are the jolly sailors of the rail. Perhaps they have worked together for a dozen years, in sun and sleet, skating over the icy tops of box-cars, and standing on the bridge at midnight. For this they have been promoted to the smoothest run on the road.

The conductor swings his hand-grip, and whistles as he strolls into the station and registers. "Train 41, on time." The wary watchman in the despatcher's office, who can close his eyes and see every train on his division at any moment, lights his pipe, and puts his feet upon the table, glad to know that the most important train on the line has reached its destination. Mr. H. Walter Webb, at the club, the playhouse, or at home, glances at his watch, and as he has received no notice of delay, knows that his pet train — the " Exposition Flyer " — has been delivered safely to the Lake Shore. While this was being accomplished, the one hundred and one passengers laughed, chatted, ate dinner, and went to bed.

It might be of interest to pause a little in our journey here, and give some account of how a great railroad is operated — each man going about his business, and doing what he has to do with so little noise.

The Superintendent of Motive Power and

Machinery has full charge of the rolling-stock — the road's equipment. The officers immediately under him are the Division Master Mechanics, who are assisted by a travelling engineer, who goes about seeing that the men as well as the locomotives do their work. He is usually promoted from an engineer, and is a valuable officer, seeing that engineers do not abuse their engines or waste the supplies. Often, upon the recommendation of the travelling engineer, firemen are promoted.

Every man reports to his immediate superior — the fireman to the engineer, the engineer to the Division Master Mechanic, he to the Superintendent of Motive Power. These officers and men are in the Motive Power Department; they are in the Operating Department also.

At the head of the Operating Department is the Division Superintendent. This officer appoints the train-masters, yard-masters and station agents. It is usually with his indorsement that brakemen are promoted to be freight conductors, and freight conductors to passenger runs. The engineer, especially when on the road, is responsible to the Division Superintendent.

Next in importance is the Traffic Department. If the road has a General Traffic Manager, the work will be in the hands of a General Freight and a General Passenger Agent. Neither the section boss, the local agent, nor the conductor can issue transportation complimentarily.

There are also the Engineering, the Auditing, Track, and Medical Departments. There is a Superintendent of Bridges and Buildings. There is the General Store Keeper, in charge of all building material and supplies. Every pound of waste, every gallon of oil, every nut or bolt, is charged to the locomotive for which it is requested; and at the end of the month the Master Mechanic knows what each engine has cost the company; how many miles she has made to the ton of coal, the pint of oil, and the pound of waste. So, you see, there are other records an engineer must make besides a record for fast running.

The conductor is the captain of the train, and as long as he is consistent his talk "goes." In addition to his duties as collector of revenue, he must, especially on a single-track road, read and check up the register, to see that all trains due, and having rights over his train, are in. If we except the despatcher, the conductor is the best judge of orders in the service. By the use of two carbon sheets, the operator receiving an order for a train will make three copies : one to file in the telegraph office, one for the conductor, and one for the engineer. The conductor will examine the order, and, if it is correct and proper, sign his name and the name of the engineer. He should go to the head end and read the order to the engine-men. If the brakemen hear it, so much the better. It would be a good plan if all these men were furnished with a copy of the order. The conductor now returns to the train. The engineer does the running ; but if he should run contrary to orders, the conductor may pull the automatic air valve and stop the train.

The writer of a recent article says : " It may be possible to make such mechanical improvements as will permit a rate of one hundred miles an hour ; but where are the men who will run these trains of the future when they are built ? "

This reminds me of a conversation which took place in my hearing thirteen years ago, in the shadow of the Rocky Mountains. The men talking were a train crew, waiting on a side track for the Leadville express, which had just begun to operate between the carbonate camp and Colorado's capital.

"They are going to build a line over Marshall Pass to Salt Lake," said the conductor; "but I 'll husk punkins 'fore I 'll run a train there."

"You think you would," said the long, lank brakeman, taking the stem of a black clay pipe from between his teeth. "I want t' tell you that if they build a road to Pike's Peak, they 'll be men just fool 'nough to go there and railroad."

In less than three years these very men were running over the mountain, and in less than ten years we saw a railroad to Pike's Peak. It makes no difference to these fearless fellows where the road runs — up a tree or down a well — so long as there are two rails. Bring on your thunder birds; never yet in the history of railroading has an engineer asked for more time. When the running time between New York and

Chicago is fifteen hours, the engine-men will work harder for promotion than they do now. We have now not only the men to run these trains, but we have the motive power. With a track as nearly perfect as engine 999, for example, herself is, she will make her one hundred miles an hour. This locomotive is the plain single-cylinder, eight-wheel type of engine, which has been a favorite with engine-men for the past fifteen years. Manifestly, Mr. Buchanan has very little faith in the newer compound locomotives which have been claiming the attention of managers of late. The Rio Grande Western, one of the swiftest little lines in the West, has been making a thorough test of the compound engine. It finds that with an ordinary train they show no saving of fuel, but with a heavy train they perform beautifully.

When the next new ocean-steamer is placed upon the Atlantic, she will probably shorten the time from Queenstown to New York to five days. That would be six days to Chicago, and seven days from Queenstown to the summit of Pike's Peak. There is no excuse for squandering five days in a journey from New York to San Francisco. This would make a comfortable time-card : —

New York to Chicago . . .	19 hours
Chicago to Denver	23 hours
Denver to Ogden	19 hours
Ogden to San Francisco . .	23 hours

Total, eighty-four hours, or three days and a half, from New York to the Pacific Coast. The same time can be made going east; for actual running time is reckoned, no allowance being made for difference in time. A sleeping-car attached to the Union Pacific fast mail leaves Omaha every evening at 6.30, and arrives in Denver at 7.30 the next morning, — five hundred and sixty-five miles. This run is made across the plains, where the traffic does not justify the expenditure of a very considerable amount of money on track. There is never a night that this train does not reach the speed of a mile a minute. Every day this fast mail-train makes the run from Chicago to Denver in a little over twenty-four hours.

Either the Rio Grande or the Santa Fé, in connection with the Rio Grande Western, can take you from the Queen City of the Plains to

Ogden in nineteen hours. The Southern Pacific has a very good track and splendid equipment, and they should be ashamed to take thirty-six hours of a short life to run a little over nine hundred miles. They can make the run in twenty-three hours, and do it easily. What we want is better track. The locomotive of to-day will do for some time.

We want, also, a high regard for the lives of passengers on the part of railroad officials and employees. Much as I would like to, I am unable to offer a reasonable excuse for some of the collisions which have cost so many lives. It was not to be expected that the railroads could handle the multitudes to and from the World's Fair without injuring a number of people, and without some loss of life. But if every section of a train had been kept ten minutes behind the section it followed, there could have been no rear-end collisions such as we have heard of recently. Every train should have proceeded upon the theory that it was followed closely by a special, and the flagman should have been instructed to flag without ceasing. Better be in Chicago ten

minutes late than in eternity ten years ahead
of time.

A locomotive should never cross the turn-
table without a box of sand, and the driver
should see that the pipes are open. Enough
sand to fill the sailor hat of a summer girl will
often save a whole train.

Of course there will always be wrecks as long
as mortal men tend the switches and hold the
throttles, for it is human to err; but the mind
should be on the work at all times. No man
should be compelled, or even allowed, to remain
on duty more than twelve hours, or eighteen at
the most. After twenty-four hours the eyes
become tired; after thirty-six hours the brain is
benumbed.

I have been on a locomotive forty hours, and
all desire to sleep had left me; but I felt that I
was dreaming with my eyes wide open. The
fireman had to speak twice to get my attention.
I was not asleep, but my mind was away, and
when called to note a signal it returned reluc-
tantly. The brain seems to feel the injustice
of such abuse, and simply quits — walks out.
Of course, it can be compelled to work, but it

will not work cheerfully or well. Just as any other striker may be forced to submit to a decrease in wages or an increase of hours, so it may work, but will "soldier" enough to put its employer on the losing side.

After such a strain I have gone to bed at eight in the evening, and have rolled and tossed and beat about until midnight, unable to sleep. Once I dozed for a few minutes, and then sat up in bed, pulled my watch from under my pillow, held it to the open window where the full moon fell upon its face, and said, so loud that I was wakened by my own voice: "Nine fifty-five ; No. 10 is due here at 10.1." Half asleep, I had dreamed that I was on the side track at Chester, waiting for the east-bound express. How forcibly the time-card rules are photographed upon the brain ! Even in my sleep I was "in to clear" six minutes before the opposing train was due.

It so happened that the night-train from Leadville was due in Salida at about that time. I could hear it roaring down through Brown's Cañon, and then I heard the long, wild wail of the whistle echoing along the sides of the

Sangre de Cristo range. I saw the head brakeman open the switch, dropped out on the main
line, saw the signal from the rear-end when the
switch was closed, and drifted away down the
valley of the Gunnison — to the vale of sleep.
A yard engine screamed for brakes — that
short, sharp shriek that tells of danger and
hints of death. I looked out of the window,
and saw the great white quivering head-light
bearing down upon me. Twice in reality I
have stood in the shadow of death, and I know
that at such times the mind sweeps over a
quarter of a century in a second or two. We
were on the side track ; our train was standing. Some one had left the switch open, and
the express was heading in upon us. There
was nothing to do but to leap for life. As
I threw my feet out of the window to jump,
the cold air awakened me, and I saw before
me, not a head-light, but the big bright moon
that was just about disappearing behind the
mountains.

And this is the way I slept until 6.30, when
the caller came. I signed the book, and at
7.30 was on the road again.

Where there are no regular runs, and the men run "first in, first out," it is almost impossible to always have just work enough to go round. The men are as much to blame as the management for the overwork of engineers. They are paid on these mountain roads four dollars per day. Days are not measured by hours, but by miles. Forty-four mountain, or eighty-five valley miles is a day on freight. On passenger service one hundred and five valley miles is a day's work. The point between valley and mountain mileage is passed when the grade exceeds two hundred feet to the mile. Men have made sixty days in a month on these mountains, and they have earned the two hundred and forty dollars; but they should not have been allowed to do it.

One young man, Hyatt by name, used to threaten to put himself into a receiver's hands when he made less than forty days a month. Fifty days was fair business, but sixty suited him better. He kept it up for three years, collapsed, and had to be hurried out of the country. I don't know that he ever wholly recovered. He was a fine fellow physically,

sober and strong, or he would have collapsed
sooner. I am afraid the older engineers are a
little selfish. When the management proposes
to employ more men, or promote some fireman, there is usually a protest from the older
runners.

In the general instructions printed in the
New York Central time-card, we find the following: "The use of intoxicating drink on the
road, or about the premises of the corporation,
is strictly forbidden. No one will be employed,
or continued in employment, who is known to
be in the habit of drinking intoxicating liquor."
They might have added "on or off duty,"
just to make it plain and strong. A man who
was drunk last night is not fit to run a train or
engine to-day. Men who never drink should
be encouraged, and promoted ahead of those
who do. I have always opposed the idea of
promoting men strictly in accordance with the
length of time they have served in any capacity.
If all firemen knew that they would be promoted when they had fired a certain number
of years, there would be nothing to strive for.
They would be about as ambitious as a herd of

steers who are to be kept until they are three
years old, and then shipped.

The best engine-man has been a fireman;
the best conductors are made of brakemen;
the best officials are promoted from the ranks.
Mr. John M. Toucey, General Manager of the
New York Central, was once a trainman. President Newell, of the Lake Shore, used to carry
a chain in an engineering corps on the Illinois
Central. President Clark, of the Mobile and
Ohio, was a section man; afterwards a fireman.
Another man who drove grade stakes is President Blockstand, of the Alton. Allen Manvill,
the late president of "the longest road on
earth," was a storehouse clerk. President Van
Horne (Sir William now), of the Canadian
Pacific, kept time on the Illinois Central. A
man named Towne, who used to twist brake-
wheels on the Burlington, is now Vice-President
Towne, of the Southern Pacific. President
Smith, of the Louisville and Nashville, was a
telegraph operator. Marvin Hughitt, of the
Chicago and Northwestern, began as a telegraph
messenger-boy. President Clark, of the Union
Pacific, used to check freight and push a truck

on the "Omaha platform." The Illinois Central, I believe, has turned out more great men than any other road. President Jeffrey, of the Denver and Rio Grande, began in the Central shops, at forty-five cents a day. General Superintendent Sample, of the same Company, began at Baldwins at $1.50 a week.

But this has been a long détour, and my wait at Buffalo was really a very short one. The 896 gave place to the 293, and in a few minutes we were under way again.

The locomotives used by the New York Central were designed by Mr. Buchanan, Superintendent of Motive Power. They consume a tank of coal over each division, and drink up thirty-six hundred gallons of water an hour, or nearly a gallon a second. A number ten monitor injector forces the water from the tank into the boiler. When I stepped from the Central's magnificent hundred-ton locomotive to the Lake Shore's little McQueen, with her five-foot-ten wheel, the latter looked like a toy.

I had not heard so much of the Lake Shore and Michigan Southern, over whose line we were now to travel, and was agreeably surprised to find such splendid track. The 293 put a mile a minute behind her with a grace and ease really remarkable. The lamps have all been blown out in the farmhouses, and the world has gone to sleep. The big white moon, that came up from the Atlantic as we were leaving the metropolis, is dropping down in the west.

The Lake Shore is remarkable for its short divisions and long tangents. "That's the east-bound 'Flyer,'" said the fireman, as a bright head-light showed up in front of us; and in a minute she dashed by. I had just begun to get used to the bell when we stopped at Erie on time.

A flat-topped Brooks locomotive, number 559, with a big, roomy cab, a youthful driver, a six-foot wheel, and an enthusiastic fireman who knew his business (as they must on this run), backed up to our train. "You 'll have this class of engine all the way to Chicago," said the engineer. "They were built for these trains." They are but little heavier than the McQueen, but splendid "steamers," good riders, and run like a coyote. The fireman found

time to show me the home of the dear dead
Garfield, and made me shudder when he pointed
to the Ashtabula bridge, where so many lives
were lost some years ago. I was glad to think
that wooden bridges and poor roadways were
things of the past.

We are making a mile a minute. What
would the driver do if he saw before him a
burning bridge, or the red lights of a standing
train? His left hand is on the throttle; he
would close it. Almost in the same second his
right hand would grasp the sand lever, and
with his left he would apply the brakes. With
both hands, in about the third second, he would
reverse the engine. Perhaps he has heard that
old story that to reverse a locomotive is to
increase her speed — that a bird will fly faster
with folded wings : he may pretend to believe
it ; but he will reverse her just the same. If
she has room she will stop. Even without the
aid of the air-brake she will stop the train, if
the rail holds out. I ought to say that, the
instant he reverses the engine, he will kick the
cylinder cocks open — otherwise he may blow
off a steam-chest or a cylinder head.

The engineer will risk his life to save his
train. Of this the travelling public may rest
assured. Even though he may be, or may
have been, the greatest coward living, a man
who has run a locomotive for a number of
years will do, in the face of a great danger,
just what I have described. To say that he
does this mechanically is not to accuse him
of cowardice. It is harder to enlist than to
march to the music and keep up with the crowd
when the battle is on. He does not, mechanically, say good-by to loved ones, and step into
the cab knowing that he must face danger, even
death. The mother seeing her child fall in
front of a cable-car, without stopping to reason
what is best to do, or taking thought of the
risk, springs to the rescue. The engineer, seeing an open switch, reasons no more, but does
that which human instinct tells him to do. It
was my business, for a number of years, to read
and write about railroad people; and if an
engineer ever left the cab without first making
an effort to save his train, I have failed to hear
of it.

Having met and passed the east-bound

"Flyer," we have absolute right of track to Chicago. All north or east bound trains have rights of track over trains of the same or inferior class going in the opposite direction. The terms passenger or freight are descriptive, and do not refer to class. All trains are designated as regular or extra. The regular trains are those on the time-cards; the extras are run by special telegraphic orders, and always carry white flags or white lights on the locomotive. An extra train composed of passenger cars is usually called a " special ; " of freight cars an " extra ; " and they must always be kept off the time of regular trains of whatever class.

" And this is Cleveland," said I, as I looked from the roomy cab of another Brooks, " the home of the Grand Old Chief? " I had hoped, by showing that I knew Mr. Arthur, to put myself in touch with the driver ; but a prophet is never appreciated at home, and the only reply was a good-natured grunt and a sarcastic smile.

It is hard pounding out of Cleveland, and I wonder that a yard-engine does not give us a little start. It is almost morning now.

Just the time for a wreck. More collisions,
I believe, occur between the hours of two and
six A. M. than in the other twenty hours of the
day. Now for the first time I feel just a little
tired. Just once I closed my eyes, and it
seemed to rest them so that I kept them closed
for a moment, until I felt myself swaying on
the seat. Then I opened them wide, for we
were making more than a mile a minute, and
to sleep was to run the risk of falling out of
the open window at my left. That was the only
time on the whole trip that I felt the least incli-
nation to sleep.

At Toledo we changed engines and train
crews, and in the gray dawn of morning pulled
out for Elkhart, Indiana. The 94 had seen
considerable service; she was not very beautiful, and, having a flat spot on one of her wheels,
was a little lame. The hostler " slid " her, the
fireman said; but when the serious-looking
engineer got her headed down the sixty-eight
mile tangent, the flat spot and the little limp
gave us no more trouble. The speed was so
great that she touched only the high places,
and the ride down the long stretch of straight

track was a delightful one. The sun, that I
had seen drop down behind the Catskills, as
it seemed, but a few hours ago, swung up
from the Atlantic, and shone on the Hoosier
hills, "where the frost was on the punkin, and
the fodder in the shock." The trainmaster,
from Toledo, came over to ride with me, and
showed me where the daring train robbers held
the train up in an open prairie, on a straight
track. We held our watches on the 94, and
found that she made ten miles in eight minutes,
and eleven miles in eight and one half minutes.
Old and lame as she is, she manages to limp
over eight thousand miles a month, at an
average rate of a mile a minute..

The 94 reminded me of a jack rabbit. When
he gets up he is so stiff and lame that a well-
trained greyhound is ashamed to chase him.
He will wabble about, stumble and fall, put
down three and carry one, until the dog is
ready to eat him. Then he lays his ears down
along his spine, and skims over the sage-brush
with the speed of the wind.

At Elkhart the 160 backed on to our train.
The conductor came running forward with a

manifold order, and, handing a copy to the
engineer, they both began to read. "Put up
green signals," said the driver; and the fireman planted a small green flag on either side
of the front end of the locomotive, and we were
off for Chicago. These flags did not affect
us or our train; they only showed that something was following us with the same rights
that we enjoyed. As often as we passed a train
or switch-engine, the engineer sounded two
long and two short blasts of the whistle, and
the other engineers answered with two short,
sharp whistles, saying that they understood the
signals.

The 160 was an easy rider, and as she slipped
down the smooth steel track, the run over the
last division was no whit less glorious than was
our midnight ride on the Central.

The cheerful driver appeared to regard his
day's work as a pleasant morning ride down
to Chicago, one hundred and one miles, in two
hours. When we were acquainted, and he had
seen my old worn license as a locomotive
engineer, he called me over to his side. Find-
ing myself, for the first time in my life, at the

throttle of a locomotive making a mile a minute,
I was almost dizzy with delight. Fields and
farms flew by, and the mile-posts began to get
together like telegraph poles. A prairie hawk
flying down the track became bewildered, and
barely saved his life by a quick swerve as the
front end of the locomotive was about to strike
him; his wing brushed the signal lamp on my
side. Little brown birds, flying in front of us,
dashed against the cab windows, fluttered from
the running board, and dropped to the ground
dead.

While she was making her mile in fifty to
fifty-five seconds, the train inspector came over
the tank, bearing a tray which held a steaming
breakfast for the "dead-head," in the cab.
"Put it on the boiler head," shouted the engineer; and then I learned what the flat top was
intended for. Placing the tray on top of the
boiler, I stood up in the corner of the cab and
ate my breakast, and enjoyed it at the rate of a
mile a minute and a dollar a meal.

Looking back along the side of this remarkable train, I was surprised to note that the
heavy Wagner cars, owing to hydraulic buffer

equipment, swayed not to exceed two inches
out of a straight line when we were making
seventy-five miles an hour.   I have never travelled in the cars of this swift train ; but, judging
from the way the locomotives ride, the coaches
must be as easy as a sleigh.   We placed the
coffee cup outside the tray on the jacket, which
is almost as smooth as glass, and it rode there
for a half hour, when the inspector took it off.

Nobody ever heard of a person drowning on
air, and yet I believe it is possible.   When we
were running at the rate of seventy-five or
eighty miles an hour, I closed my mouth and
leaned out of the window.   The force of the
air was so great that it actually strangled me ;
I tried it again and again, with the same result.
The air drove into my nostrils with such force
that I invariably opened my mouth to breathe ;
and then the air drove down my throat, and
compelled me to draw back into the cab.   Now,
when we breathe water into the nostrils, we
always throw open the mouth, only to take in
more water and strangle the worse.   If, when
you had put your head out of a locomotive cab
moving at seventy-five or eighty miles an hour,

a strong hand seized it and held it there, you would, I believe, actually drown.

In California they do not say the oldest mission, the largest orchard, the biggest tree " in the State " or " in the Union," but "in the world." I shall say this is the swiftest and safest long distance train on earth. That it is the swiftest, the time-card proves. It is the safest, for the reason that, from the moment the " Exposition Flyer " leaves New York, every man in the employ of the New York Central and the Lake Shore railroads, including Dr. Depew and Mr. John Newell, look out for her until she whistles into Chicago. If the " Flyer " loses over five minutes, the fact as well as the cause of the delay is wired at once to Mr. Edgar Van Etten, the General Superin-- tendent. Everything is out of the way, and switches set for her ten minutes before she is due. Ordinarily, when a passenger train is late, her danger is correspondingly increased. Not so with the " Exposition Flyer ; " she has the right to the rail until she is able to use it, or until she becomes twelve hours late. When she is one minute late, all who are watching and waiting for her know it, and their anxiety increases until she is heard from.   No train on the road runs closer to her time-card than the " Flyer."   Nearly all the ugly wrecks are rear-end collisions ; but there is no danger from that source to this train.   Nothing short of a thunder-bolt can catch her.

But, behold, here in full view are the glisten-ing domes of the White City and the mammoth, high-mounted Ferris wheel ! The last of nearly a thousand miles of steel has slipped from under our faithful steed, and at precisely ten o'clock A.M. we stop at the Chicago station — on time. It has taken twenty hours, eight engines, and sixteen engine-men to bring us through, and it has been a glorious trip — the best of my life.

The Death Run

THE DEATH RUN

A LONG in the early eighties, when the Denver and Rio Grande was a narrow gauge road, and the main line lay across the great divide at Marshall Pass, there was a wreck in the Black Cañon, and of that wreck I write.

So rough and impenetrable was this cañon that the men sent out to blaze the trail were unable to get through. Engineers, with their instruments, were let down from the top of the cañon wall, hundreds of feet, by long ropes; and to this day, if you look up when the train goes round " Dead Man's Curve," you will see a frayed-out rope whipping the gray rocks, five hundred feet above the river and the rail.

By the breaking of this rope a human life was lost : the first of many lives that have been lost in this wild cañon. In the rush and hurry to complete the road, little attention was given

4

to sloping the cuts or making it safe for the
men who ride ahead. So, when spring came,
and the snow began to melt on the mountains
and moisten the earth, great pieces of " scenery "
would loose their hold upon the steep hill, and
sweep down the side of the cañon, carrying
rails, road-bed, in fact everything but the right
of way, across the river, where the land-slide
was often landed high and dry on the opposite
shore.

So often was the " scenery " shifted during
the first twelve months that the night run
through the Black Cañon, so wildly beautiful
by day, so grand and awful by night, came to
be called the " Death Run."

It was engineer Peasley's run out that night ;
but he had just returned from the stony little
graveyard that had been staked out on the
banks of the Gunnison, where they had buried
his baby. He was a delicate-looking man, and
when he came into the round-house that afternoon to register off, he wore his soft hat far
down over his inflamed eyes, as if he would
hide from the world any trace of that sacred
grief. Kipp, his fireman, saw him, and was

sorry, for he knew how dearly the driver had loved the little one now lost to him. Sliding from the pilot, where he had been scouring the number-plate, Kipp went to the book and registered off also.

And so it happened that, when Number Seven left Gunnison at 9.15 Jack Welsh held the seat, and fireman McConnell handled the scoop. The sharp exhausts from the straight stack sent up a solid stream of fire, as they hurried out through the yards, that fell like hail among the crippled cars on the " rep" track.

The brisk bark of the bounding engine dwindled down to à faint pant, and was drowned in the roar of the wheels, as the long train hurried away down the valley, and was swallowed up in the Black Cañon. The run was regarded as a difficult one ; but the extra crew were equal to it, and at every station up to 11.30 the operator wired the despatcher, the despatcher the train-master, and he the superintendent : "Number Seven on time."

Although he had no regular run, McConnell was really an old fireman. He had but recently returned to the road after a year's absence.

At the earnest solicitation of his good mother, he had left the rail to return to his father's farm near Salina, Kansas.   He was a good and dutiful son, and he loved his mother as only such a son can love ; but he could not help the longing within him to return to the road.   That summer the Missouri Pacific opened a new line right through his father's farm, and every day he heard the snort of the iron horse, saw the trains go to and fro, saw the engine-men throwing kisses to the girls on the farm, and he wanted to return to the Rockies.   More than once every day he looked away to the west, where he knew the trains were going up and down ; where the snow lay in great drifts on one side of the track, and the flowers bloomed by the other.   Who can say how the heart of the engine-man longs for the engine ?

> He loves the locomotive
>   As the flowers love the lea,
> As the song-birds love the sunlight,
>   As the sailor loves the sea.

When the harvest had been cut and the golden grain garnered, the restless youth bade his parents adieu, and set his face toward the

sunset. He had been a faithful fireman, and
found no trouble in re-establishing himself in
the service of the "Scenic" Line.

The Death Run was a long one : one hundred
and thirty-five miles over mountains and through
cañons. They had crossed Cero summit, and
were now roaring along the cañon, by the banks
of the beautiful river.

The night grew warmer as they drifted down
toward the valley of the Grande. The engineer
sat silently in his place, trying the water, whistling for stations, and watching the way. The
fireman, having little to do now, lounged in the
open window and looked out on the rippling
river where the moonlight lay. It was almost
midnight when the operator at Roubideau was
awakened by the wild wail of the west-bound
express. As the long train rattled over the
bridge beyond the little station, the operator
reached for the key and made the wire say :
" Number Seven on time."

Beyond the bridge there was a bit of a tangent, a few hundred yards ; and when they
turned into it, the fireman got down from his
comfortable seat to fix the fire.

The driver released the brakes at the bridge, and the train was now increasing her speed at every turn of the wheels. Looking ahead, the engineer saw the open mouth of Roubideau tunnel, which, being on the shadow side of the hill, looked like a great hole in the night. Nearer the engine he saw a number of dark objects scattered about. In another second he discerned what these were, and realized an awful danger. As he reversed the engine and applied the air, he shouted to the fireman to jump. He might have jumped himself, for he saw the danger first; but no such thought came to him. In another second the pilot was ploughing through a herd of cattle that were sleeping on the track. If they had all been standing, he would have opened the throttle and sent them flying into the river, with less risk to his train. But they were lying down; and as they rolled under the wheels, they lifted the great engine from the rails and threw her down the dump at the very edge of the river. So well had the faithful engineer performed his work that the train was stopped without wrecking a car. Many of the passengers were not awakened.

The trainmen came forward and found the engineer. He was able to speak to them; he knew what had happened, and knew that he had but a few minutes to live. These brave, rough men of the rail never hide anything from each other, and when he asked for his fireman, they told him the fireman was dead.

As he lay there in the moonlight, with his head resting in the conductor's lap, while the brakeman brought a cup from the mail-car and gave him a drink of water, he told them where he wanted to be buried, — back East somewhere; spoke of his insurance policy; left a loving message for his wife; and then, as if he had nothing more to say or do, closed his eyes, folded his hands over his brave heart, and without a murmur — apparently without pain — died.

It was many hours before they found the fireman. When the crash came, he was standing in front of the furnace door. The tank doubled forward and forced him up against the boiler-head, where, if he had not been killed instantly, he must have been slowly roasted. He lay in the wreck so long that, when they got him out, there was a deep and ugly groove across his face, where he had lain against the narrow edge of the throttle lever. Save this deep furrow, there were no marks upon his face. But that one mark remained, even after the body was embalmed.

The writer was, at that time, employed by the same company, and was sent out to the wreck to take charge of the body of the fireman, bring it to Denver, and then take it back to the farm at Salina. The travelling engineer went out with a special engine and the superintendent's private car, and I went with him.

It is not a pleasant task to deliver the dead to bereaved relatives; but it is the least that can be done, and some one must do it. The engine left the track precisely at midnight, Friday night, and it was not until the afternoon of the following Tuesday that I reached Salina.

There had been six children in this happy family, three boys and three girls. The eldest son was a locomotive engineer, but he had left the road for good, and was now with the family at the Kansas farm.

"How does he look?" asked the engineer, when we had taken seats in the farm carriage. "Can mother see him?"

"He looks very well," said I; and then, remembering that ugly furrow in his face, "but would it not be better for all of you to remember him just as he left home?"

"I shall leave that all to you," he said, while the hot tears fairly rained down upon the lap-robe that covered our knees.

When we reached the McConnell place, and I went into the house where the family were all assembled in the large, plain parlor, there was no need of an introduction. They all knew me, and knew why I had come, and when they crowded about me, all weeping so bitterly, I felt that I could not hold out much longer myself. I did better than I had expected, however, until I attempted to talk, when the tears came up in my throat and choked me. So, with a little brother on one knee, a little sister on the other, while the two young ladies were sobbing by the window, and the brave young engineer was trying between his tears to calm his mother, I gave way, and wept with the rest.

When we had all gained the little relief that always comes with a shower of tears, the mother began to talk to me and ask questions. To begin with, she asked me if I could tell her exactly when her boy was killed.

"Last Friday night," I said.

"What time?" she asked, glancing at her two daughters, who had turned from the window, and were trying to dry their eyes.

"Almost exactly at midnight," was my reply.

"Ah!" she said, bursting into tears again, "I knew it! I knew it!"

"He was killed instantly," said I; "he never knew what happened."

I said this with the hope of their deriving a shade of comfort from the fact that the dear, brave boy was not roasted alive, as so many engine-men are.

"Not quite instantly," said the weeping mother. "He called me twice: 'Mother! Mother!' and I saw him standing before me with a great deep furrow across his face."

Then she placed the edge of her hand against her face to show me where the scar was; and when I saw her mark the very angle of the ugly

groove, I felt a strange tingling sensation at the
roots of my hair.

" Has any one written you the particulars of
the wreck?" I said.

"No," she answered, " we have had but two
telegrams : one from the superintendent, telling
of his death, and the one from you when you
left Denver."

What she said so affected me that I excused
myself and walked out to the barn, where I
could think. I was not long in arriving at the
conclusion that when the 177 left the track, in
that infinitesimal fragment of time, the boy saw
that he was in the shadow of death, and his first
and only thought was of his mother. His whole
soul went out to her so swiftly and so surely
that she not only heard him call her, but saw
him, just as he was.

At the barn I found the dead boy's father,
who had insisted upon his son's going in with
me, upon our arrival at the house, while he
" put up " the team. I thought his the saddest
face I had ever seen, as he moved about in his
tearless and silent sorrow.

" How did it happen?" asked the farmer,

when he had finished his chores, and we were walking back toward the house together.

" Hit a bunch of cattle," said I.

" In the night ? "

" Yes," was my answer, " just about mid-night."

" What night ? "

" Last Friday."

"Stop," said the farmer, touching my arm. " I want to tell you something that happened here last Friday night — and I remember that it was just about midnight."

Then he told me how his wife had screamed and wakened him, and how she had wept bit-terly, and insisted that Johnny had been killed. He had been struck by somebody or something, she insisted, and she could see a great deep, ugly scar on his face.

I don't know why I did not ; but I remem-ber distinctly that I did not tell them — not even the engineer, who was accustomed to see-ing such things — that the scar was there, on Jack's face, just as his mother had seen it that Friday night.   We did not open the coffin at the church, nor at the grave.

I remained with the family at the farmhouse that night, and with them, on the following day, went to the little church in town, where the good priest talked a great deal longer than was necessary, I thought, for he had it not in his power to do John McConnell any good by talking. In a pleasant place, on a gentle slope that tipped to the west, his grave was made; and while we were weeping there, another grave, in another place, was being filled, hiding from the eyes of the world the body of the brave engineer.

Flying Through Flames

———•———

FOREST fires had been raging in the mountains for more than a month. The passengers were peering from the car-windows, watching the red lights leap from tree to tree, leaving the erstwhile green-garbed hills a bleak and blackened waste.

The travelling passenger agent had held the maiden from Normal out on the rear platform all the way up the mountain, soothing her fears, and showing her the sights and scenes along the line. "Over there," he said, "is the sunny San Luis Valley, and those high hills — that snowy range — when seen in the golden glow of sunset was called by the Spaniards *Sangre de Cristo*, the blood of Christ. Farther to the south and a little west is the great silver camp of Creede, where it is always afternoon.

"Looking far down the vale you can see the

5

moon-kissed crest of the Spanish range, below whose lofty peaks the archaic cliff-dwellers had their homes. Here to the north, where you see the fire flying from the throbbing throat of a locomotive, is the line that leads to Leadville, whose wondrous wealth is known to all the English-speaking people ; yes, even as far south as Texas they have come to talk of Leadville and the mines.

" Now we have reached the crest of the continent, where —— "

" Oh, yes, I have seen it ! " chimed in the maiden. " It 's by Ernest Ingersoll, is it not ? "

" No," he replied, " this one is by the Builder of the universe, and, as I was about to say, the water flows this way to the Atlantic, and that way to the Pacific Ocean."

" Why, how very, very funny," said the " schoolmarm ; " but the railroad man has never been able to see where the laugh came in. He was making no attempt to be funny ; and, turning the tourist over to the porter, after assuring her, for the one-hundredth time, that accidents were never heard of on Marshall Pass, he said good-night.

The conductor came out from the smoky station, lifted his white light a time or two, the big bell sounded, and the long train began to find and wind its way over the smooth steel track that should lead from the hoary heights to the verdant vale. And the gentle curves made cradles of the cars, and the happy maiden in high Five dreamed she was at home in her hammock, while the man of the road went peacefully to sleep in upper Six, feeling that he had shown all the wonders of the West to at least one passenger in that train-load of people.

The engineer reached for the rope, and the long, low "toooo toooo-too toot" went out upon the midnight air; and the women folks whispered a little prayer for the weary watcher in the engine cab, placed their precious lives in his left hand, and went to sleep again. The long train creaked and cracked on the sharp corners, and as the last echo of the steam-whistle died away in the distant hills, slid swiftly from the short tangent, and was swallowed up by a snowshed.

At that moment the fire leaped from a clump

of pinions, and the sun-dried snowshed flashed aflame like a bunch of grass in a prairie fire.

It had required the united efforts of three locomotives to haul the train up the hill, and the engineer knew that to stop was to perish in the fire, as he was utterly unable to back out of the burning building.

That is why it appeared to the passengers that all at once every tie that bound this human-burdened train to the track parted, and the mad train began to fall down the mountain. Away they went like the wind. On they went through the fiery furnace like a frightened spirit flying from the hearth of hell. The engine-men were almost suffocated in the cab, while the paint was peeled from the Pullman cars as a light snow is swallowed by the burning sun on a sandy desert.

At last the light is gone; they dash out into the night, — out into the pure mountain air; the brakes are applied, the speed is slackened, the women are still frightened; but the conductor assures them that the danger is past.

Now they can look back and see the burning sheds falling. The " schoolmarm " shudders as she climbs back to her berth, and an hour later they are all asleep. At Gunnison they get another locomotive, a fresh crew, and the train winds on toward the Pacific slope.

The engine is stabled in her stall at the round-house. The driver walks about her, pats her on the neck, and talks to her as he would to a human being: "Well, old girl, we got through, did n't we? But it was a close call."

A Novel Battle

A NOVEL BATTLE

SNOW–BUCKING with a pilot plough is dangerous business. However, there is very little of it to do in these days. Now a road that is able to accumulate a snow-drift is able to own a rotary plough or snow excavator. These machines are as large as a coach and as heavy as a locomotive. The front end is funnel-shaped ; and instead of throwing the snow away it swallows it, and then spurts it out in a great stream like water from a hose at a fire. Inside the house, or car, there is a boiler as large as a locomotive boiler, with two big cylinders to furnish power to revolve a wheel in the funnel-shaped front end. This wheel is like the wheel of a windmill, except that the fans or blades are made of steel and are quite sharp. As the plough is driven through the drifted snow by a locomotive, — sometimes by two or three of them, — the rapidly revolving wheel slices the snow from the hard bank, draws it into the steel chest, where the same rotary motion drives it out through a sheet-iron spout.

Once at Alpine Pass, on a summer branch of the Union Pacific, I saw one of these machines working in six feet of snow that had been there six months, and was so hard that men walked over it without snowshoes. It was about the middle of May; the weather was almost warm at midday, but freezing at night. A number of railroad and newspaper men had gone up there, eleven thousand feet above the sea, to witness a battle between two rival excavators. The trial was an exciting one, and lasted three days. Master Mechanic Egan, whose guest I was, was director-general, and a very impartial director, I thought. The two machines were very similar in appearance ; but instead of a wheel with knives, one had a great auger in front, the purpose of which was to bore into the snow-drift and draw the snow into the machine, as the chips are drawn from an auger hole by the revolving of the screw. The discharging apparatus was similar in the two, and like that already described.

There was a formidable array of rolling stock on the two sidings at the foot of the mountain where we had our car and where we camped nights. On one side track stands one of the machines, with three engines behind her; on another, the other, with the same number of locomotives. You could tell the men of the one from those of the other, for the two armies dwelt apart, just as the Denver police kept clear of the State militia in Governor Waite's war.

It was perfectly natural for the men on the different machines to be loyal to their respective employers, and a little bit jealous of the rival crew; but I was surprised to see how quickly that feeling extended to the crews of the half-dozen locomotives, all working for the same railroad company, and in no way interested in the outcome.

On the morning of the first day of the trial, when the six engines came down the track from the coal-yards, a trainman stood at the three-throw switch, and gave a locomotive to each of the two machines alternately. They all knew where they belonged, and they kept the same place, each of them, until the battle was over.

There was no betting, but there was a distinct "favorite" from the start; and when the iron horses were all hooked up, the men on the "favorite" began, good-naturedly enough, to "josh" the other crew.

Mr. Egan decided that one of the machines should go forward; and when it stuck, stalled, or stopped, for any reason, it should at once back down, take the siding, and give the other a chance.

It was nearly noon when the railway officers and pencil-pushers climbed to the storm deck of the first machine, and the commander gave a signal to start. The whistle " off brakes " was answered by the six locomotives, and the little engine that brought up the rear with the special train. The hungry machine gathered up the light drifts which we encountered in the first few miles, and breathed them out over the tops of the telegraph-poles. At a sharp curve, where there was a deep drift, the snow plough left the track, and we were forced to stop and back out. The engineers looked sullen as they backed down to let the other crew pass, and the fresh men laughed at them. The snow was lighter now, so that instead of boring into it, the second plough only pushed it and piled it up in front of her, until the whole house was buried, when she chocked up and lay down. Now the frowns were transferred to the faces of the second crew, and the smiles to the other.

For two days we see-sawed in this way, and every hour the men grew more sullen. The mad locomotives seemed to enter into the spirit of the fight; at least, it was easy to imagine that they did, as they snorted, puffed, and panted in the great drifts. Ah, 'twas a goodly sight to see them, each sending an endless stream of black smoke to the very heavens, and to hear them scream to one another when about to stall, and to note with what reluctance they returned to the side-track.

In the little town at the foot of the hill the rival crews camped at separate boarding-houses. This was fortunate, for it would not have been safe for them to live together. Even the engine-men by the end of the second day were hardly on speaking terms. Bob Stoute said that somebody had remarked that the 265 would n't make steam enough to ring the bell. He did not know who had said it, but he did know that he could lick him. After supper that evening, when the "scrappy" engineer came out of Red Woods saloon, he broadened the statement so as to include "any 'Rotary' man on the job, see?"

When we went into the field on the morning of the third day, not more than seven miles of snow remained between us and the mouth of the Alpine tunnel, where the race would end, for the tunnel was full of snow. All the forenoon the hot engines steamed and snorted and banged away at the great sea of snow that grew deeper and harder as we climbed. The track was so crooked that the ploughs were off the rail half the time; so that when we stopped for luncheon we had made less than three miles.

The least-promising of the two machines was out first after dinner; and as the snow was harder up here, she bid fair to win great credit. She rounded the last of the sharp curves that had given us so much trouble successfully.

But as the snow grew deeper she smothered, choked up, and stalled. Then even her friends had to admit that, " she was not quite right," and tne engine-men looked blacker than ever as they backed down and took the siding.

Up came the rival, every engine blowing off steam, the three firemen at the furnace-doors, the engineers smiling, and eager for the fray. As she turned into the tangent where the other had stalled, the leading locomotive screamed " off brakes," and every throttle flew wide open. Down, down went the reverse levers, until every engine in the train was working at her full capacity. While waiting in the siding, the engineers had screwed their " pops," or relief valves, down so that each of the engines carried twenty pounds more steam than usual. There were no drifts now, but the hard snow lay level six feet deep. The track was as good as straight,— just one long curve ; and the pilots would touch timber line at the mouth of the tunnel. The road here lay along the side of the mountain through a heavy growth of pine. The snow was granulated, and consequently very heavy. By the time they had gone a hundred yards, a great stream of snow was flowing from the spout out over the telegraph wires, over the tops of the tall spruces and pines, crashing down through their branches until the white beneath them was covered with a green carpet of tree-twigs. On and on, up and up, the monster moguls pushed the plough. Higher and higher rose the black smoke ; and when the smoke and the snow came between the spectators and the sun, which was just now sinking behind the hill, the effect was marvellously beautiful. Still, on they went through the stainless waste, nor stopped nor stalled until the snow plough touched the tunnel-shed.

The commander gave a signal to " back up ; " and with faces wreathed in smiles, and with their machine covered with cinders, snow, and glory, the little army drifted down the hill. The three days' fight was at an end, and the Rotary was the victor.

But I started to write about pilot ploughs and old-time snow-bucking, — when we used to take out an extra insurance policy and say good-by to our friends when we signed the call-book. On a mountain division of a Western road, some ten years ago, I had my first experience in snow-bucking. For twenty-four hours a pilot-plough and flanger had been racing over the thirty miles of mountain, up one side and down the other. As often as they reached the foot of the hill they received orders to "double the road."

It was Sunday afternoon when the caller came for me. Another engine had been ordered out to help push the snow-plough through the great drifts, that were getting deeper and deeper every hour. Ten miles out from the division station, at the foot of the mountain proper, we side-tracked to wait the return of the snow-plough.

The hours went by, the night wasted away. Monday dawned, and no news of the snow brigade. All we could learn at the telegraph office was that they were somewhere between Shawano and the top of the hill, — presumably stuck in the snow. All day and all night they worked and puffed, pushed and panted, but to no purpose. Now, when they gave up all hope of getting through, they attempted to back down; but that was equally impossible.

The heavy drifts in the deep cuts were not to be bucked away with the rear end of an engine.

Tuesday came, and found us still watching and waiting for the snow plough. Other engines came up from the division station with a work train, and a great army of trackmen with wide shovels. A number of railroad officers came, and everybody shovelled. We had no plough on our side of the hill, and had to buck with naked engines. First we tried one, then two, then three coupled together. The shovellers would clear off a few hundred yards of track, over which we would drive at full speed. As our engine came in contact with a great drift, all the way from eight to eighteen feet deep, she would tremble and shake as though she was about to be crushed to pieces.

Often when we came to a stop only the top of the stack of the front engine was visible. The front windows of the cabs were all boarded up to prevent the glass from being smashed. For three or four days the track was kept clear behind us, so that we could back out and tie up at night where there was coal and water.

All this time the snow kept coming down, day and night, until the only sign of a railroad across the range was the tops of the telegraph poles. Toward the last of the week we encountered a terrific storm, almost a blizzard. This closed the trail behind us, and that night we were forced to camp on the mountain side. We had an abundance of coal, but the water in the tanks was very low; but by shovelling snow into them when we were stuck in the deep drifts, we managed to keep them wet.

For three or four days — sometimes in the dead hours of the night — we had heard a mournful whistle away up on the mountain side, crying in the waste like a lost sheep. This was a light engine, as we learned afterward, that had started down the hill, but got stuck in the storm. For four days and nights the crews were imprisoned in the drifts. They had only a few pieces of hard bread, which they soaked in snow water and ate. More than once during the fourth day they had looked into the tallow bucket, and wondered if they could eat the tallow.

On Sunday morning, just a week from the

day on which I had signed the call-book, the sun shone clear and bright. The crew with the big pilot plough had reached the summit; and now a new danger confronted the lone engine, whose cry had gone out in the night like the wail of a lost soul. The big plough was coming down the hill with two locomotives behind her; and if this crew remained on the main line, they would be scooped into eternity. When the storm cleared away, they found that they were within a few feet of the switch target. If they could shovel out the snow and throw the switch, it would let them on to a spur. Hungry and weak as they were, they began with the fireman's scoop to clear the switch and shovel away from the wheels so that the engine could start herself. All the time they could hear the whistles of the three engines, now whistling down brakes, back up, and go ahead, as they hammered away at the deep drifts. At last the switch was forced open, the engine was in to clear; but not a moment too soon, for now came the great plough fairly falling down the mountain, sending a shower of snow over the lone engine on the spur.

We, too, had heard and seen them coming, and had found a safe siding. When the three half-starved and almost desperate engineers came to the clear track we had made, the great engines, till now held in check by the heavy snow, bounded forward down the steep grade at a rate that made us sick at heart. Each of the locomotives on the side track whistled; but the wheels were covered with ice and snow, and when they reversed their engines they seemed to slide as fast. Fortunately, at the next curve, there was a heavy drift, — so deep that the snow-train drove right through it, making a complete tunnel arched over with snow. Thus, after eight days, the road was opened, and eight sections of the passenger train came slowly and carefully down the mountain and passed under the arch.

On Board an Ocean Flyer

ON BOARD AN OCEAN FLYER.

AT midnight seventy-two fires were lighted under the nine big boilers of the "Bismarck," and shortly after a cloud of yellow smoke, rolling from the huge stacks, was floating over the bosom of the bay.

In their various homes and hotels a thousand prospective travellers slept and dreamed of their voyage on the morrow.

By daybreak the water evaporating into steam fluttered through the indicators, and as early as 6 A. M. people were seen collecting about the docks, while a fussy little hoisting engine worked away, lifting freight from the pier. At seven a few eager passengers came to the ship's side, anxiously inspecting her, and an hour later were going aboard.

Officers in uniform paced the decks, guarded the gangways to keep intruders back, and others of the crew, in citizens' clothes, mingled freely in the crowd, having a sharp eye for suspicious characters.

Finally, the steam-gauge pointer advances to the hundred mark. Noise and confusion wax wilder. The ship's crew is busy, from captain to meanest sailor, until at ten o'clock, thirty minutes before sailing, the sound of hurrying feet is lost in a deafening hum of human voices. All visitors are now refused admittance, except perhaps a messenger with belated letters, packages, or flowers for people on board.

The little hoister fairly flies about in a heroic effort to lift everything that is loose at one end and store it away in the ship's hold. The pier is invisible, buried beneath a multitude of peering people.

All being ready, the captain is notified, and at his signal the first engineer pulls the lever and starts the little engine whose work it is to open the throttle, the steam shoots out from the big boilers into the great cylinders, screws begin to revolve, and the ocean-liner, with one thousand passengers, two thousand tons of coal, and three thousand pounds of ice cream, leaves the landing.

Hundreds of handkerchiefs flutter, and hundreds of people say good-bye, with eager, upturned faces that try to smile through tears. Some are sad with the pain of parting, while others, like Byron, are sad " because they leave behind no thing that claims a tear."

Thirty-six stokers take their places before the furnace-doors, each with two fire-boxes to feed. There are three stoke-holes, twelve men in each, and twelve buckets of cold water, with a bottle of red wine in every bucket. As the speed increases, the great ship begins to rise and fall ; not with the swell of the sea, for there is no swell and no sea, but with her own powerful exertion.

When the ventilators catch the ocean breeze and begin to drink in the salt air, there is rejoicing in the stoke-room. Unfortunately for the stokers, the increased draught increases also the appetite of the furnaces, that seem famishing for fuel.

After four hours in the heat, semi-darkness, and dust of the furnace-room, the stokers come out, and fresh men with fresh bottles take their places. Gradually the speed of the boat increases. The fires are fanned by the ever-increasing breeze, the furnaces fairly roar, and the second shift work harder than the first.

If there is no wind, instead of allowing the stokers to drop dead, the engineer on watch simply turns a lever and starts the twelve large steam fans, and saves the firemen just before the bone buttons are melted from their overalls.

The steamship stoker is inferior mentally to the locomotive fireman, but physically he is the better man. The amount of skill required to stoke is nothing compared to that of firing a railway engine. The locomotive fireman must use his own judgment at all times as to how, when, and where to put in a fire. The ocean stoker simply waits for a whistle from the gang-boss, when he opens his furnace-door, hooks, rakes, and replenishes his fire, and at another signal closes the doors, the same whistle being a signal to his brother stoker at the other end of the boiler to fix his fire.

The white glare of the furnaces when the fires are being raked is so intense that the place seems dark when the doors are closed. And through that darkness comes the noise of the rattling clinker-hooks, the roar of the fires, the squeak of the steering-engine, and the awful sound of the billows breaking on the ship. Once above all this din I heard a stoker sing:

> "Oh, what care we,
> When on the sea,
>   For weather fair or fine?
> For toil we must
> In smoke and dust
>   Below the water-line."

Then came the sharp whistle, and the song was cut short as the stoker bent to his work, and again the twenty-four furnaces threw their blinding glare into our faces.

With all the apparatus for cooling the stoke-room, it is still a first-class submarine hell.

One night, when the sea was wicked, rolling high and fast from the banks of Newfoundland; when the mast swung to and fro like a great pendulum upside down, — I climbed down to the engine-room. When the ship shot downward and the screws went out of the water, the mighty engines flew like dynamos, making the huge boat with her hundreds of tons tremble till the screws went down into the water again.

In the stoke-rooms the boilers lie crosswise

of the ship; so when she rolls it is with the greatest difficulty that the stoker prevents himself from being shot head first into one of the furnaces. Here I watched these grim toilers this wild night, and it seemed the more she rolled, pitched, and plunged, the more furiously they fed the furnaces. What with the speed of the ship and the speed of the wind, the draught was terrific, and the fire boxes seemed capable of consuming any amount of coal that could be thrown into their red throats. Though absolutely safe, the stoke-room on a night like this is an awful place for one unused to such scenes; so terrible that a young German, working his way from New York to Hamburg, was driven insane.

As the sea began to break heavily on the sides of the boat and make her rock like a frail leaf in an autumn wind, the man was seen to try to make his escape from the stoke-hole. For an hour he worked in the same nervous way, always looking for a chance of escape. At last the ship gave a roll that caused the furnace-door to fly open, and with the yell of a demon the green stoker sprang up the steps leading to the engine-rooms. Here one of the engineers, seeing the man was insane, blocked the way. The poor fellow paused for a moment, and stood shaking like an aspen, while the cold perspiration rolled down his face. Two or three men tried to hold him, but, without the slightest effort, apparently, he cast them off, and, running out on the steerage deck, jumped into the sea.

All through the night, above the roar of the ocean, at regular intervals, came the sharp whistle of the head stoker, and at longer intervals the cry from above: "All's well." On Sunday morning when we awoke, the waves still washing up the steerage deck and the great ship rolling from side to side, we could hear from the stoke-room the same shrill whistle, and the same cry outside of "All's well." Then, like a flood of sunlight, came the sweet strains of the anthem, which the band always plays on Sunday mornings; and again the sea came up and closed our windows and shut out the light of day, and the sound of the sea drowned all other sounds, and seemed to suggest "Nearer My God To Thee." The waves rolled back, the sun shone in through the window, and the hymn was heard again.

When the reckoning was taken, we were all surprised to learn that on such a tempestuous sea this wonderful ship had made a mile more than on the previous day on a summer sea.

" Look away," said the captain, as we passed an ocean steamer that seemed to be standing still.

" Is she at anchor? " I asked.

" No," said the captain, "she 's making twelve knots an hour; and only a few years ago she was one of the ocean greyhounds."

Within the last decade the time between New York and Southampton has been reduced by nearly two days; but those who look for a like reduction within the next ten years will surely be disappointed. The Lucania, with thirty thousand horse-power, is able to make only a little over a mile an hour more than the Fürst Bismarck, with sixteen thousand. If by nearly doubling the horse-power, and with twenty-five per cent more firemen, we can shorten the time but half a day, then indeed does the problem become a difficult one.

The Fürst Bismarck is 502 feet long, 27 feet wide, and 60 feet deep, from her hurricane deck to her keel. There are nine huge boilers, 15 feet 7 inches in diameter, and 19 feet long. It requires 130 stokers and trimmers, and 300 tons of coal a day to keep them hot. They boil down 100 tons of water every 24 hours. There are, all told, 55 engines on board the ship. The steam that drives the boat passes through three pairs of cylinders. The first are 43 inches in diameter, and work at a pressure equal to eleven atmospheres. The next, 67 inches, working at four atmospheres. The third are the low pressure cylinders, 106 inches in diameter, with one atmosphere pressure, and a vacuum equal in working power to an atmosphere.

There are two main shafts, one to each screw, or propeller, 20 inches in diameter, each 142 feet long, and weighing a ton for every foot of steel.

There are twelve engineers and twelve assistants. Over all these men there is a chief engineer, whose duties are similar to those of a master mechanic on a railway. His office is a little palace, finished in beautiful Hungarian ash, supplied with easy-chairs and soft couches. There is an indicator which shows at all times the pressure under which the various engines are working and the speed of the boat.

When we were ready to go below, the chief engineer pressed a button, which, he explained to us, was a signal to the engineer in charge to open the doors and allow us to pass from one room to another ; for there are water-tight doors between the engines. There are in all thirteen air-tight compartments, so that if a man-of-war were to stave a hole in one side of the Bismarck, that compartment would simply fill with water, but would do no serious damage. In fact, a half-dozen holes might be stove in, and she would continue to ride the waves.

If the Bismarck were to strike a rock and cave in six feet of her bottom or keel, a solid plate or false bottom would then be reached that would stand almost any pressure.

When a boat with a single propeller loses her steering apparatus, she is in great danger ; but with a twin screw ship there is absolutely no danger. By simply reversing one screw, the ship may be steered as a row-boat is guided, by holding one oar still, and moving the other.

The electric-light plant alone is of interest. There are four dynamos, and they supply a current for eighteen hundred lamps. In addition to the lamps in the saloons and state-rooms, all the signal-lights are electric, as well as the lights used in the steerage and in the supply rooms.

The chief steward has been with the company twenty-seven years, and will probably be there as long as he cares to remain. There are eighty-four other stewards, who report directly or indirectly to him. The passengers are divided into three classes, — first cabin, second cabin, and steerage ; so that three separate and complete kitchens and dining-rooms are kept up. The food furnished for the steerage passengers is better than one would expect when we consider that the company carries them from New York to Hamburg and keeps them on board seven days for $10.

The food and service in the second cabin are better than at the average $3 a day American hotel. In the first cabin saloon they are perfect. The stewards file in in regular order, and

when a change is made they all march out,
keeping time to the band, and making, with
their neat uniforms and snow-white gloves, a
goodly sight to see.

Each table has its own table steward, and at
the elbow of each passenger stands a white-
gloved under-steward who seems capable of
anticipating your very thoughts. If a drop of
coffee is spilled over your cup — before you
have time to realize it yourself — both cup and
saucer are exchanged for one in perfect trim.

The regular dinner consists of from seven to
ten courses, and is fit for the Emperor. The
wines and ales are excellent, and are forty per
cent cheaper than in New York.

In addition to the regular meals, at eight
o'clock every evening they serve tea in the main
saloon to all who care to indulge in that stimu-
lant. After that, at nine o'clock, the band
gives a concert in the second cabin saloon,
which is always attended by many of the first
cabin passengers. There, the people sit about
the tables and eat the daintiest little sand-
wiches, and some of them drink the delightful
Hamburg beer, while the band plays.

If you are ill and remain in your berth, the room steward will call a half-dozen times a day to ask you what you want to eat. If you remain on deck, the deck steward will bring you an excellent dinner without any extra charge.

It was the day after the rough sea when we were shown through the steerage; the women and children were still huddled in their gloomy bunk-rooms, recovering slowly from the sea-sickness of the previous day.

Cheerless as their surroundings were, they had the satisfaction of knowing that the countess at the top was as sick, when she was sick, as they.

Forward, where the ship's side walls are close together, the sailors sleep. Here, when the sea is rough, one may experience the sensation of riding in the elevator of a sixteen story building, and, as the bow descends, the sensation of falling. The occupants of this rough quarter are a rough-looking lot, but apparently as happy as cowboys. Every sailor has his regular ration of rum, while the stokers, in addition to the red wine they have in the stoke room, have kümmel four times a day.

Just back of the sailors are the stores. In the cold room, where the meats are kept, all the pipes are covered with frost. The large ships all have ice-machines, and make their own ice. There are also two large evaporators, so that if the supply of drinking water should become unfit for use, drinking water could be made from the sea. The same evaporators could easily supply water in the same way for the boilers, should the supply run short.

Two things I should like to change : the tons of wholesome food, delicious meats, and delicate sweets that are carried from the tables and thrown into the sea, I would give to the poor steeragers. Every day at dinner, when the lamps made the saloon a glare of light, I could see these poor people peeping in at the windows, where the tables were freighted with good things, and it made me sad. Sometimes a mother would hold her poor, pinch-faced baby up to the window; and I could not help wondering what answer that mother would make if the baby were to ask why they did n't go in and eat.

After making the steerage happy, I should like to rig a governor to the main shafts, so that the screws would not " cut up " so when out of water.   I mentioned this to Mr. Jones. He looked at me steadily for a moment, then, as he allowed his head to dip slightly to the starboard, a sunny smile broke over his kindly face, and he replied, " Well, somebody has tried that already."

On an Iron Steed

HUNDREDS of hansom cabs, countless carriages, and myriads of omnibuses came out of the fog and filled the ample grounds in front of Victoria Station. A solid stream of men, women, and children was pouring in at the gates to the platforms where the trains stand. Long lines of people were waiting in front of the windows in the booking office. Trunks, bags, and boxes fairly rained into the luggage-room; but the porters (short, stout fellows) picked them up and bore them away, as red ants run away with crumbs at a picnic.

To the train, titled people came in carriages, behind splendid horses, with coachmen in high hats, and footmen in yellow trousers. American millionnaires came also in coaches and tally-hos, and mingled with the plain English nobility.

You can tell the American women by their smart dresses, and the English by their heavy boots, red cheeks, and heaps of hair. You can tell the London swell from the New Yorker, for there is something the matter with one of his eyes. And you can pick out the duke and the lord, for they are, in most cases, plain and modest men. There is a noticeable absence of poor people; for the train is not going to the hop-fields of Kent, but to Paris and the Riviera. The American representative of the London, Chatham, and Dover Railway, in a shining silk hat, a snow-white cravat, and blood-red boutonnière, and the station-master, are busy assigning small parties of Americans to compartments, and larger parties to saloons. The Englishman travelling in his native land makes little trouble for any one. He usually has his luggage aboard and his porter dismissed with a scowl and a threepence, while the foreigner with a smile and a shilling awaits his turn. All the Englishman asks is to be let alone; and surely that is not too much.

The faded carriages that stretch away in a long line towards the locomotive look singularly small to those who are accustomed to seeing the heavy trains of America.

And now we come to the locomotive. The stoker touched his cap when I stepped aboard, and I noticed that he did this every time he addressed me. If I asked a simple question he invariably touched his cap before he answered.

The absence of a pilot, or " cow-catcher," as it is sometimes called, makes the English locomotive look awkward and unfinished to an American. There are no cylinders, cross-heads, or main rods in sight, and at a first glance she reminds one of a well-made stationary engine. Even her beautiful high wheels are half covered with steel. Like a well-dressed Englishman, the English locomotive looks best from her knees up.

Above her running-board she is scrupulously clean, bright, and interesting. But even here she has a vacant look. There is but one steam dome and no sand box or bell; she looks as though she had been driven under a low bridge and had her back swept bare, and then had nothing rebuilt but one dome and the stack.

In the cab, where ought to be comfortable seats for the driver and stoker, there are high boxes that come nearly to the window sills. No matter how long he remains on duty, the driver must stand up ; nor has the stoker, who in descending a long bank might get a moment's rest, any place to sit, but must stand the whole way on his weary feet. This is simply disgraceful. The precious lives of thousands of people are placed in the hands of the engine-driver, and yet no thought is given to his comfort. I read, with considerable amusement, an article in an English journal urging ·the Board of Trade to provide medals as a reward to engine-drivers "for duty ably done." I would suggest better wages, and seats in cabs. Medals are all right as a mark, but even titles are no good when we are dead. Think of a man spending years in learning a trade, and then doubling the road between London and Dover, a hundred and sixty miles, for seven shillings, —$1.75, or ninety miles for a dollar, —just $3 less than an engineer gets for covering the same distance on a mountain road in the United States. The risk is about the same, for an English driver runs four times as fast as the mountaineer.

Out through the ragged edge of London, over the Thames, and down the rail our steel steed whirled us at a rapid rate. The English driver does not run "with his hand on the throttle, and his eye on the road," as we are wont to picture a locomotive engineer; for the throttle is at the top of the boiler head, and must be sought out by the driver before he can shut off steam, no matter how great the emergency. It does not require a practised railroader to understand that if the driver had his hand on the lever, he could shut off without taking his eyes from the rail, and in less than a quarter of a second.

Five miles out we stopped at a small station, and picked up four more carriages. Our train was equipped with the matchless " Westinghouse " air-brakes; and they do the work delightfully on these light cars. So perfectly were they adjusted, and so smoothly did the quiet old seven-shilling-a-day driver apply them, that the train came to a dead stop with as little jolt as would attend the stopping of a baby carriage.

Already I had learned to like our locomotive; but when we got a signal to go, and the driver gave her steam, the fifteen carriages refused to start. Here I witnessed, for the second time in my life, the working of the slowest, clumsiest piece of machinery in use to-day in any civilized country, — the " reversing wheel." I had seen it once before, when the London and North-Western's prize engine was leaving Chicago. When the locomotive fails to start her train, it is always necessary to reverse her to get what there is of slack between the cars. In this way the engine starts a car at a time, so that by the time the last car is started, the locomotive has made a quarter of a turn or more, and the front part of the train is in motion. With a quick-working reverse lever this is accomplished easily ; but with a wheel that must be given from seven to eleven revolutions to reverse the machinery, the process is painfully slow, without the saving grace of being sure. As the wheel revolves, the locomotive creeps forward, stealing the slack from car after car, so that by the time the machinery is in the forward motion the slack is gone, and you are just where you were before you began to reverse. There was a serious collision on the Great

Northern not long ago; a double-head express train dashed into a goods train that was being shunted; and if the locomotive had "wheels," the wonder is that more people were not killed.

From Herne Hill, where we got the last four carriages, it is seventy-five miles to Dover; and we were to make the run without a stop. Just about the time our steed got them going, she dashed into a tunnel half a mile long. The great drivers hammering the rails, and the rattle of the carriages, made a deafening roar, and, to add to the torture, the driver pulled the whistle. The English locomotive whistle is the shrillest, sharpest, most ear-splitting instrument of torture ever heard. It is about as musical as a Chinese fiddle accompanied by a lawn-mower.

As the smoke of London began to grow dim in the distance, a beautiful panorama of fields and farms opened up before us. As far as the eye could reach on either side were rolling meadows and brown fields, dotted with thatch-roofed stacks. If the speed slackened as we ascended a long "bank," these rural pictures claimed my attention and made me forget for

8

the moment that we were at the front of the
Paris express. But when we had reached the
summit, and the world began to slip beneath
us till the keen air cut our faces, we were made
to realize that we were not losing any time.
Now we were rolling along the top of a high
hill, from whose flat summit we looked down
the chimney-pots in the village houses; and
now dashing into a deep cut, where flocks of
frightened quail rose up and beat the bank,
or, caught by the eddying wind, were dashed
against the sides of the flying train, as a man
standing near the track and grown dizzy throws
himself beneath the wheels.

A sharp curve throws our train out on the
brow of a gentle hill. Below, through a green
valley, winds a lazy looking river — the Med-
way. This is the old town of Rochester, the
land of Dickens, and beyond the river stands
the old Norman castle.

And this is what Mr. Jingle said when he
saw it : —

" A fine old place — a glorious pile — frown-
ing walls — tottering arches — dark nooks —
crumbling staircases — old cathedral, too —

earthy smell — pilgrims' feet wore away the old steps — little Saxon doors — confessionals, like money-takers' boxes at theatres — queer customers, those monks — popes, and lord treasurers, and all sorts of old fellows with great red faces and broken noses turning up every day — buff jerkins, too — matchlocks — sarcophagus — fine place — old legends — strange stories."

The red vines that cling to the shoulders of this rare old ruin glow warmly in the autumn sun. Only a flash, and we turn another corner, and the old castle is lost in the dreary blond brick houses of Rochester. Now and then, as the train whirls through the city, the towering spires of the cathedral are seen.

Away, away, the engine flies, and the dull town is left for the sunny fields. We are now entering the great hop fields of Kent, — one of the fairest counties in all England, I am told. Ours is not the only locomotive abroad, for almost every moment we can see another train flying across the country, always crossing either above or below our track. Out in the fields are other engines, great awkward machines pulling ploughs, and sometimes trains of wagons, through village streets. At the end of a long curve, around which we swing at a mile a minute, rise the great spires of the cathedral of Canterbury.

Here, too, are clinging vines and crumbling walls, old legends and strange stories. Here are stone steps worn away by pilgrims' knees, — the steps that lead from the musty crypt to Becket's shrine. Here sleep the murdered Bishop and the King. But there is no time to dream, for we are now whirling away towards the water-edge. At last the driver shuts off steam, the stoker washes the deck with a water-hose connected with the injector pipe, and remarks that his work is done. His labor, like his salary, is light; for although we have been on the road nearly two hours, he has not burned a half-ton of coal. The trains, of course, are light, and that makes light work for the engine-men. It is all down hill now, and we fairly fall through the tunnels and deep cuts, till all at once the " silver streak," as they call it here, is seen ; and this is the end of the first heat.

Many things bear the name of " the widow

at Windsor," and I was not surprised to find the Victoria rocking restlessly by the dock at Dover. It is surprising to an American to see how quickly fourteen English carriages can be emptied. I should say that in two minutes from the time our train stopped, we were all aboard. In eight minutes the baggage was transferred from the train to the boat, and in ten minutes we were leaving the dock.

The Channel has not the reputation of being particularly pacific, and this was one of her busy days. In ten minutes after the whistle sounded, the Victoria was capering out towards the coast of France just as an untamed broncho capers with a cowboy across a corral. To the disgrace of the London, Chatham, and Dover Railway Company, she is a side-wheeler. Except the reversing-wheel and the seatless cab of the 117, this is the only disgraceful thing I found on the Dover route.

There are in the Victoria a number of state-rooms, a splendid lounging saloon, a ladies' cabin, and a "public house." Better than all these things, there are the ever-ready stewards, who watch the women; and just at the moment when life loses its glitter, and the unhappy tourist ceases to care, come quietly, wearing the while a look of deepest sympathy, leave a small regretting basin by her chair, and move away.

I made a short study of a lord going over. He was not what you would call distinguished looking, in his large soft hat and rain coat, but he looked respectable at least. We had not gone very far when he began to turn his head from side to side as if he had lost something. Then he would close his eye for a spell, and try to think. He was the homeliest man I have seen in Europe; and he was constantly doing "stunts" with his good eye in order to keep the glass in the other. I don't know whether he died or not, for a sort of malarial feeling came over me, and I lost interest in everything except the French coast.

In spite of the rough sea, we made the run from Dover to Calais, twenty-five miles, in a few minutes over an hour.

"Chemin de Fer du Nord" is the first French sign seen by the voyager from England. It is the name of the railway — or "road of iron," as the French put it — over which we are to pass to Paris.

The captain of the Victoria had given me a letter which contained a pass, — a "permis de monter sur les machines," — and this pass went on to say that I would be "permitted to circulate or promenade on the machine drawing the quick express during one voyage between Calais and Paris."

Sliding back into my engine clothes, I went forward to where the locomotive stood steaming and sizzling, ready to be off.

Just as I reached her, the driver began to whirl the reversing wheel; for he had heard the signal-bell, and the long train moved away. I showed my pass. The driver smiled, and waved me out of the fireman's way. The cab was the same wretched, comfortless cavity that I had seen on the Dover, only not so clean. The tank, or tender, where the coal is carried, was filled with slack and dust. As fast as he shovelled into the heap where the slack was dry, the fireman turned the hose on it, until it was a puddle of mush; and, to my surprise, he shovelled this slop into the firebox, and kept the locomotive howling hot. It would be impossible, of course, to fire an American express locomotive with such fuel; for there the engines are worked so much harder to draw heavy trains. When we had whipped around a few curves I saw that the best place for me was behind the driver, and I stepped over to his side.

There existed between the engine, the engine-men, and me a feeling of estrangement that was almost melancholy.

I missed the sleepy panting of the air-pump, and the click of the latch on the reverse lever. There was no bell to relieve the monotony of the rasping, phthisicky whistle. I wondered if we could ever understand each other, if she would respond to my touch; for the driver talked to her in a strange tongue.

The engine-men wore no gloves, and handled the door-chain and hot levers as though they were wood. The driver held a piece of burning waste in his hand to furnish fire for his cigarettes. I did not reproach him or blame him for smoking cigarettes; it was the " wheel," no doubt, that drove him to it.

If cabs had seats, running a locomotive would be much easier in Europe than in America. The ways are all walled or fenced in, and there is no necessity for the constant straining of the eyes and nerves, from which American drivers suffer so much.

The first stop is at Amiens, eighty miles out. There I saw what I had never seen before, — women working the switches in a signal-tower. There were two of them, and they appeared to have the station quite to themselves. I make no doubt that they find their work very agreeable and interesting, that they are faithful, that their homes are happy, and that they consider themselves very superior, and refuse to exchange calls with their sister, the " bullwhacker."

At Amiens we met Night on her way to the west, and I gave up the engine for the more comfortable carriage. This compartment was very like the one assigned our party on the Chatham and Dover, except that it was a trifle wider, and done in tan instead of blue.

Here, as in England, the stations are ample, with all the tracks under cover. The trains stop but five minutes; but the European car-

riages soon discharge their passengers, — the
first-class into the *buffet*, the second, as a rule,
into the *buvette*. A brass-hulled yard engine
was hustling about, uttering shrill shrieks in the
great sheds. The yard-men worked without
lamps, and wore horns over their shoulders,
through which they " conched " signals to the
engineers. The locomotives have no head-
lights in Europe, such as are used in the States,
but there was a hand-lamp, or a lightning-bug,
chained fast to the pilot of the " shunter " at
Amiens.

After trembling away in the twilight for an
hour, and an hour into the night, the street-
lamps began to thicken by the way, and in a
few minutes we stopped in the great station
of the Nord, and were in Paris.

Over an Earthquake

OVER AN EARTHQUAKE

FOR more than twenty minutes the cab rattled through the narrow, stony streets of
Paris, crossed the Seine, always interesting, but
weirdly beautiful at night, with its many bridges
and countless lamps of every color, and finally
stopped at the Gare de l'Est.

"Orient Express, Monsieur?" asked the porter, as he balanced my box on the scales.

"Oui," said I ; and then he cried the weight,
—fifty kilos. "Twenty-one francs, if you
please," said the man in the baggage-office, and
I flashed up my transportation.

"Twenty-one francs," the money-taker repeated, and I showed my sleeping-car ticket,
thinking I had him on the hip this time sure.

"For the baggage, for the baggage," he said,
in French, growing impatient ; and I gave him
the money. Manifestly there was no free bag-

gage on the Orient Express; and the rate of twenty-one francs, 1 7*s*. 10*d*., or \$4.20 for one hundred pounds, eight hundred miles, was a stiff one.

To the porter who freighted my trunk I gave some sous, and saw him drop them into a locked box at the door of the baggage-room. In England the porters keep what they get, and it has a good effect. It makes the individual porter look out for baggage; for the more people he serves, the more he will receive. In France each porter waits for the other, knowing the division will be equal at night; and so there is nothing to work for. It kills competition, this French arrangement, and makes the man almost worthless. The moment you relinquish the " pourboire," the porter's interest in you ceases. He simply heads you in on the main platform, where you must work out your own salvation. I fancy this rule does not apply at all stations, but it certainly does at the Gare de l'Est, with a very bad result.

The train which I was preparing to board this bleak November night consisted of a smart-looking locomotive and five cars. Next

the engine there was a sort of combination express, baggage, and commissary car, where the
stores were kept. Then came the dining-car,
one-third of which was made into a beautiful
smoking saloon, with great easy-chairs put up
in dark leather. Back of the diner there were
three sleeping-cars, Mann boudoirs, and running along under the roof, above the tops of
the high windows, in bold gold letters, was the
name of the company unabridged, "The International Bed-Wagons Company and the Grand
European Express;" only it was in French, and
ran like this: "Compagnie Internationale des
Wagons-Lits et des Grands Express Européens."

The outward appearance of this company's
trains is similar to the trains run on the American continent. The cars are long, and rest on
eight wheels. You enter the car at or near the
end, and pass through a narrow corridor, from
which you enter the compartments. A compartment holds two or four people, and often,
with the judicious expenditure of a few francs,
the voyager can secure a small compartment all
to himself, and he is quite as secluded and comfortable as he would be in the state-room of a

Pullman or Wagner. There are certainly many advantages in a compartment sleeper. A man travelling with his wife has only to provide himself with two tickets and secure a compartment all to themselves. Two ladies travelling together would have the same advantage.

There is no rush or excitement, no one appears to be in any hurry. Three or four porters come along, leisurely rolling a little iron car containing a small canvas travelling-bag. Other porters — not in uniform — come with hot-water cans, — long flat cans which they slide into the compartments of ordinary European coaches; but the Orient is heated by steam. Now comes a truck with a great many mail-bags, which are put into the rear car. The mails are an important item to the railways, and as this train leaves Paris but twice a week, they are usually heavy. In half an hour the splendid train is trembling away in the night. It is seven o'clock, and the dining-car is filled with people, — men and women from every corner of the earth. If a Russian speaks to an Italian, or a German to a Spaniard, it is almost invariably in French.

All the reading matter belonging to the train is printed in three languages; but only French is spoken, save when another language is absolutely necessary. The cards posted in the cars have these headings: "AVIS," "NOTIZ," "NOTICE."

The dining-car service is equal to the best in any country, and the rates are reasonable. The first breakfast is the regulation European bill, — bread, butter, and coffee, with fruit if you want it, for 1 f. 75 ¢ (1 s. 5 d., or 35 cents).

At eleven o'clock they serve a good *déjeuner* for five francs, — a dollar, — and at evening a splendid dinner for six francs; so you have three good meals for $2.55, which in America, in the average dining-car, would cost three dollars.

When dinner is over, the men lounge in the smoking-room for a couple of hours, and then go to their 'boudoirs.'

In a few hours we were rolling away toward the selvage of France over a smooth track. Shortly after midnight I was awakened by a commotion at my door, opened my eyes, and beheld an officer in the corridor. He was

9

grand beyond description. With every movement of the train he flashed back to me the
flickering light that went out of my compartment to his plated person. In addition to the
cord on his cap and his brilliant buttons, he
wore festooned about his breast enough gold
cable to rope a steer; and I knew then that
we were in Germany. This awe-inspiring individual stood without, while his assistant, a less
imposing personage, inspected my ticket and
hand-luggage.

We left Paris at 6.50 P. M., and at noon the
next day we were at Munich. Half-way between
noon and night we were rolling along the banks
of a beautiful river, near the edge of Austria.
It was a clear, sparkling stream such as run
rapidly down from the hills, and far to the
south we could see the mountains wearing
their first white robe of winter, and stabbing
the blue sky with their polished peaks.

When the train stops at a station of any
importance, an officer with a large book, followed by two or three assistants, goes to the
locomotive, secures the autograph of the engineer, and gives him a lot of vocal instructions.

They all talk at once, "kracking" their *k*'s till one is reminded of a skating party breaking through the ice. Finally peace is declared, they all salute, and the train moves on. Everything has a military air about it. The old woman sweeping a crossing brings her broom to her shoulder, and the one-legged watchman comes to the proper position, with a red flag for a musket, as the train goes by.

Twenty-four hours takes the traveller to Vienna, 1,402 kilomètres, — over 800 miles, — which is very good speed.

The locomotives used in Austria are more like American machines than those of England and France, and the day-cars are the best I have seen on the Continent. They are heavier than the ordinary European railway carriage, and rest on eight large wheels. First-class carriages are heavily padded with beautiful Russian leather, clean, cool, and comfortable. You enter these cars, not at the side nor at the end, but at the corner; the compartments open into a corridor.

Leaving Vienna, you pass through a great valley, or prairie, where farmers follow bull-teams down the dark furrows that seem never to end, but disappear at the edge of the horizon. The vastness of the fields, and the houses so far apart, give the land an air of desolation.

At midnight we were at Budapest, the beautiful capital of Hungary, with a splendid king's palace on the Danube ; but there is no king there : the king is the Emperor of Austria, and lives at Vienna. Here are more strange-looking people, and the signs and notices are printed in four tongues. Twenty minutes for another language.

Dropping down the Danube for six or seven hours, we see the sun rise in Servia, and the first stop on the following day is at Belgrade.

Farther to the south, it is warmer here ; the earth is dry, and the sky clear. Here the voyager begins to feel that he is in a new world, with strange people. Here are evidences of dress reform. The pantaloon is merging into the gown, or the gown into the pantaloon, perhaps, as it is in America. Each succeeding hour takes the traveller farther into this desolate country, so old and yet so new, with so little of what are now regarded as signs of civilization.

Here prosperity and poverty appear to meet and pass. A wild-looking shepherd, in his coat of wool, gazing at the train, reminds me of the lone wolf as I have seen him stand in my native land, watching the train with nothing near him but solitude and God.

In the low, stone-fenced corrals are stacks of fine oak-brush, cut from the gentle hills, evidently in summer when the leaves were green; and this brush is to be given to the frail horses, cows, and donkeys for hay. These stacks of bushes tell more than enough of the poverty of the country. When we have travelled through it, we wonder how the International Sleeping-Car Company can afford to run a train even twice a week through such a land.

At noon we met and passed the west-bound train. It may be that we had passed other trains; but this was the first passenger train I had seen for forty hours.

I carried with me a permit to ride on the locomotive of the Orient Express when I wished to do so, and now I slipped into my engine clothes and mounted the machine. The engineer was a native; and about all we could say to each other was "Yes" and "No" in French.

Nearly, if not all, the railroads here are operated by the Governments of the various countries through which they pass. The Orient express, however, is operated solely by the Sleeping-Car Company. This company's conductor, who goes all the way from Paris to Constantinople, is the captain of the train; only the Government inspectors of the different countries come aboard to inspect baggage and look after the interest of the Government. The railway fare from Paris to Constantinople by the Orient Express, a *train de luxe*, is sixty-nine dollars; the sleeping-car ticket is eighteen dollars.

The track was only fair, but the locomotive was in good condition. The time is slow, not more than twenty or thirty miles an hour.

At the first road crossing outside the town we found a long line of wagons drawn by small cattle, waiting at the closed gate. Behind these wagons, reaching far out to the hills, miles away, were strings of pack animals loaded with corn on the stalk. Evidently this was an important market for the surrounding country.

It was a beautiful afternoon, soft as September in Paris or New York. The road here ran

up a broad vale, which, however, grew narrower
as we ascended the waterless stream. On either
side the wash, the country grew rough ; the hills
in the distance would be called mountains in
the Holy Land. The wagon road lay parallel
with the railway, and in half an hour we passed
hundreds of ox teams bringing wood down from
the hills. Some women and children were
driving a flock of turkeys, a man was leading a
sheep, and others were carrying jars of something — honey perhaps — on their heads.

All at once the air grew still ; an oppressive
silence seemed to hang on vale and hill, and
all the people stopped short. It seemed to me
that we had run into a bad piece of track, or
that our train had suddenly quickened its pace.
I saw a Servian woman, with a little child
on her arm, stagger, stop, take the water-jug
from her head, and hug her frightened babe to
her naked breast. Hundreds of yoked cattle
were lowing, burros were braying, and whole
flocks of sheep were crying on the distant
downs. Meantime the curves seemed to increase ; and although we were not making more
than forty miles an hour, we appeared to fairly

fly.   Men stood still and stared at the heavens.
A Mohammedan slid down from a pack-mule,
spread his prayer-rug, set his face toward Mecca,
and prayed.   Christians crossed themselves, and
as often as I stole a glance at the driver I found
him looking at me.   Till now, I had attributed
the action of these wild people to childish
wonder at seeing the train sweep by ; but when
I looked at the almost pale face of the sun-
browned driver, I was bewildered.   The things
I beheld were all so unnatural that I felt my
head swimming.   Glancing ahead, I saw the
straight track take on curves and shake them
out again, resembling a running snake.   The
valley had become a narrow gulch, and from
the near hills arose great clouds of smoke, as
from a quarry when the shots go off.   The fireman, who had been busy at the furnace-door,
stood up now and gazed at the driver, who
pressed his left hand hard over his eyes, then
took it off and tried to see, but made no attempt
to check the speed of the flying train.   As a
drunken cowboy dashing down a straight street
sways in his saddle, as a wounded bird reels
through the air, did this mad monster of a

locomotive swing and swim o'er the writhing rail.

Suddenly a great curve appeared in front of us. This time the stoker, who had left off firing, saw it, and made the sign of the cross. Again the driver hid his eyes, and again I felt my brain grow dizzy trying to understand. We could hear and feel the engine wheels rise and fall on the twisting rail with a deafening sound. At last she settled down, and began to glide away as a boat glides down a running stream.

"What is it?" I asked of the French fireman.

"Tremblement de terre," he said, shaking himself violently, and pointing to the ground; and then I understood that we had been riding over an earthquake. The driver was either too proud and brave to stop, or too frightened to be able to shut off steam; I don't know which.

Passing out of Servia, we clip off a corner of Bulgaria, calling at the capital, Sofia.

The next place of importance is Adrianople, the old capital of the Turks. It was here that young Mohammed caused the great cannon to be cast with which he battered the walls of Constantinople, and conquered Constantine, the last Christian emperor of Byzantium, while the fat priests plotted against each other, and the poor ignorant Christians laid down their arms to cross themselves.

It is Wednesday morning, and we are rolling slowly along over a dreary, desolate-looking country. All things European are rapidly disappearing. The old familiar battle-cry of the beggars of France, "pourboire," is changed to "baksheesh."

Instead of section men with picks and shovels, we see by the side of the track dark Turks in bicycle trousers, carrying rusty muskets on their shoulders.

Here and there, far apart, we find bands of dusky, sooty laborers burning oak-brush, from the sticks of which they make charcoal.

While we are at *déjeuner*, the train toils up a long grade, and finally reaches the summit of a sort of tableland from which we look down into the quiet Sea of Marmora, sleeping silently between Europe and Asia. It looks more like a great lake than a sea, with its sloping shores and marshy margin, fringed with flags and swamp-grass.

Now we are entering a city that seems very old. The train rolls along among the houses behind a rain-stained wall ; and when we stop, we find the platform crowded with red caps, the cabmen are having a spirited argument, hotel-runners, guides and dragomans are pushing each other, a long line of *hammels*, or porters, are waiting at the customs office, and beyond them a line of miserable beggars, and this is Constantinople.

Through the Dardanelles

———•———

CONSTANTINOPLE may be considered as
the end of the railway system of the earth.
Here, if you wish to see more of the Orient,
you must take to the sea. There is, to be
sure, a projected railway out of the Sultan's
city into the interior, but only completed to
Angora, three hundred and sixty-five miles.

The intention of the projectors was to con-
tinue the road on down to Bagdad, on the River
Tigris, through which they could reach the
Persian Gulf.

I had arranged to go to Angora, but found
a ten days' quarantine five miles out of Constantinople, and backed into town. I then
made an effort to secure from the office of
the titled German who stands for the railway
company some idea of the road, — its pros-
pects, probable cost, and estimated earnings;
but my letters returned without a line.

To show that I was acting in good faith and willing to pay for what I got, I went with Vincent the guide, — the only good guide I ever knew, — and asked them for some printed matter, or photographs, or anything that would throw a little light along the line of their plague-stricken railway; but they still refused to talk.

No wonder it has taken these dreamers ten years to build three hundred and sixty miles of very cheap railroad !

It was my misfortune to fall into a little old Austrian-Lloyd steamer, called the Daphne. Before we lifted anchor in the Golden Horn, I learned that her boilers had not been overhauled for ten years; and before we reached the Dardanelles, I concluded that the sand had not been changed in the pillows for a quarter of a century. I have slept in the American desert for a period of thirty nights, between the earth and the heavens, and found a better bed than was made by the ossified mattress and petrified pillows of the Daphne.

It was bad enough to breathe the foul air that came up from the camping pilgrims on the main deck; but the first day out we learned that these ugly Armenians, greasy Greeks, and filthy Bedouins would be allowed to come upon the promenade deck and mingle with those who had paid for first-class passage.

Poorly clad, half-starved, poverty-stricken people headed for the Holy Land came and rubbed elbows with American and European women and children. Of course, one sympathizes with these poor miserable people; but one does not want their secrets. These facts are not put here to injure the steamship company, but that other voyagers may fight shy of these little old rattle-traps of coast steamers, that ought to be run up a canal for the sea-birds to rest on. This company has many excellent steamers, and ought to be ashamed to put first-class passengers into a cattle-ship and charge first-class rates.

We left the Bosphorus at twilight, crossed the Sea of Marmora during the night, and the next morning were at Gallipoli, where the bird-seeds come from.

The day broke beautifully, and the little sea was as calm as a summer lake. By ten o'clock

10

we were drifting down the Dardanelles, which resembles a great river; for the land is always near on either side.

The ship's doctor, who was my guide at every landing-place, kindly pointed out the many places of interest.

"Those pyramids over there," he would say, "were erected by the Turks to commemorate a victory. Here is where Byron swam the sea from Europe to Asia; and over there is where King Midas lived, whose touch turned piastres to napoleons, and flounders to gold fish. Here, to the left, on that little hill, stood ancient Troy."

All things seemed to work together to make the day a most enjoyable one, and just at nightfall the doctor came to me and said, —

"See that island over there? That was the home of Sappho."

And there she sang, —

> "'T was like unto the hyacinth
>   That purpled on the hills,
> That the careless shepherd, passing,
>   Tramples underfoot and kills."

An hour later, we anchored in a little natural harbor, and five of us went ashore.

Beside the ship's doctor, — whose uniform was a sufficient passport for all, — there were in our party a Pole and a Frenchman (both inspectors of revenue for the Turkish Government, and splendid fellows), a Belgian, and the writer. We entered a café-concert, where one man and five or six girls sat in a sort of balcony at one end of the building and played at " fiddle." The main hall was filled with small tables, at which were Greeks, Catholics, Armenians, Turks, and negroes as black as a hole in the night. Between acts, the girls were expected to come down, distribute themselves about, and help consume beer and other fluid at the expense of the frequenters.

The girls were nearly all Germans, — plain, honest, tired-looking creatures, who seemed half embarrassed at seeing what they call " Europeans." One very pretty girl, with peachy cheeks, who, as we learned, had for several evenings been in the habit of drinking beer with a Greek, sat, this evening, with a dark Egyptian, almost jet black. The Greek — a hollow-chested, long-haired loafer — came in ; and the moment he saw the girl with the chalk-eyed man, turned red, then white, and then, whipping out a gun, levelled it at the girl. Nearly all the lights went out, and the girl dropped from the chair. When the smoke and excitement cleared away, it was found that the bullet had only parted the girl's hair, and she was able to take her fiddle and beer when time was called.

At midnight we were rowed back to the boat, with all the poetry knocked out of the isle of Sappho, hoisted anchor, and steamed away. On the whole, however, the day had been a most delightful one. To me there are no fairer stretches of water for a glorious day's sail than the Dardanelles.

When we dropped anchor again, ten hours later, it was at Smyrna, the garden of Asia Minor. Here I went ashore with my faithful guide, the doctor, and found a real railway. The Ottoman Railway, whose headquarters are at Smyrna, was the first in Asia Minor, and was begun by the English company, which continues to do business, thirty-six years ago. Mr. William Shotton, the Locomotive Superintendent, showed us through the shops and buildings. One does not need to be told that this property is managed by an English company, — I saw here the neatest shops and yards that I have ever seen in any country. There were in the car-shops some carriages just completed, designed and built by native workmen who had learned the business with the company; and I have not seen such artistic cars in England or in France.

Mr. Shotton explained to me that they found it necessary to ask an applicant his religion before employing him, so as to keep the Greeks and Catholics about equally divided; otherwise the faction in the majority would lord it over the weaker band, to the detriment of the service. An occasional Mohammedan made no difference; but the Greeks and Catholics have it in for each other, as they do at Bethlehem, just as they had in the dark days of the gentle Constantine, and just as they will have till the end of the chapter.

The Ottoman Railway Company has three hundred and fifty miles of good railroad, and hopes some day to be able to continue across to Bagdad, — though it is hinted by people not interested that the Sultan's Government favors the sleepy German Company, to the embarrassment of the Smyrna people, who have done so much for the development of this marvellously blessed section.

We spent a pleasant day at Smyrna, with its water-melons, Turkish coffee, and camels; and twenty-four hours later we were at the Isle of Rhodes, where the great Colossus was. It was a dark, dreary, windy night, and the Turks fought hard for the ship's ladder. We had on board a wise old priest from Paris, with a string of six or eight young priests, who were to unload at Rhodes. Despite the cold, raw wind and rain, men came aboard with canes, beads, and slippers made of native wood, — for there is a prison here, — and offered them for sale at very low prices.

For the next forty-eight hours our little old ship was wallopped about in a boisterous sea, and when we stopped again it was at Mersina, where a little railroad runs up to Tarsus, where Saul used to live. As we arrived at this place after sunset, — which ends the Turkish day, — we were obliged to lie here twenty-four hours, to get landing.

On the morning of the second day, after our arrival at this struggling little port, our anchor touched bottom in the beautiful Bay of Alexandretta. Here they show you the quiet nook where the whale shook Jonas. That was a sad and lasting lesson for the whale ; for not one of his kind has been seen in the Mediterranean since. All day we watched them hoist crying sheep and mild-eyed cattle, with a derrick from row-boats, up over the deck and drop them down into the ship, — just as carelessly as a boy would drop a string of squirrels from his hand to the ground.

The next morning we rode into the only harbor on the Syrian coast, and anchored in front of the beautiful city of " Bayroot," — I believe that is the correct spelling ; it is the only way it has not been spelled !

It would take too long to describe this place, even if I had the power, to tell of the road to Damascus, the drives to the hills of Lebanon, through the silk-farms, the genial and obliging American Consul, the American College : but here, after nine days and nights, we said good-by to the obliging crew of the poor old Daphne.

It was Christmas Eve when we learned that
the sea had quieted sufficiently to allow ships
to land at Jaffa ; and as early as 3 P. M. Cook's
comedian came and hustled us aboard. The
ship did not leave until 7.30, and we had to
pay a dollar each for our dinners. For nearly a
week the steamers had been passing Jaffa without landing, and the result was that Beyroot and
Port Saïd were filled with passengers and pilgrims for the Holy Land. All day the Russian
steamer which we were to take had been load-
ing with deck or steerage passengers, poorer
and sicker and hungrier, if possible, than those
on the Daphne were. It was dark when they
had finished, and when we steamed out of
the harbor we had seven hundred patches of
poverty piled up on the deck. It began to
rain shortly, — that cold damp rain that seems
to go with a rough sea, just as naturally as red
liquor goes with crime. For a week or more,
these miserable, misguided beggars had been
carried by Jaffa, from Beyroot to Port Saïd, then
from Port Saïd to Beyroot, unable to land. And
this was Christmas Eve. Not a passenger nor
a pilgrim in all that vast shipload but had hoped

and prayed and planned to be at Bethlehem
to-night. The good captain caused a canvas to
be stretched over the shivering, suffering mob
that covered the deck; but the pitiless rain
beat in, and the wind moaned in the rigging,
and the ship rolled and pitched and ploughed
through the black sea, and the poor pilgrims
regretted the trip in each other's laps. All
night and till nearly noon the next day they
lay there, more dead than alive; and the hard-
est part of their pilgrimage was yet before them.
If you have ever seen a flock of hungry gulls
round a floating biscuit, you can form a very
faint idea of a mob of native boatmen storming
a ship at Jaffa. Of course the ladders are filled
first; then those who have missed the ladders
drive bang against the ship, grab a rope, or
cable, or anything they can grasp, and run up
the iron, slippery side of the ship, as a squirrel
runs up a tree.

From the top of the ship they began to fire
the bags, bundles, and boxes of the deck passengers down into the broad boats that lie so
thick at the ship's side as to hide the sea
entirely. When they had thrown everything

overboard that was loose at one end, they began on the poor pilgrims.

Women, old and young, who were scarcely able to stand up were dragged to the ladders and down to the last step. Here they were supposed to "lay" for the boat into which the Arabs were preparing to pitch them; for the sea was still very rough. Now the bottom step of the ladder was in the water, now six feet above; but what did these poor ignorant Russians know about gymnastics? When the rolling sea brought the row-boats up, the pilgrims usually hesitated, while the bare-armed and bare-legged boatmen yelled and wrenched their hands from the chain. By the time the Mohammedans had shaken a woman loose, and the victim had crossed herself, the ladder was six or eight feet from the small boat; but it was too late to stay her now, even if the Arabs had wished to, — but they did not. When she made the sign of the cross, that decided them, and they let her drop. Some waiting Turks made a feeble attempt to catch the sprawling woman, but not much. Sometimes, before one could rise, another woman — for they were nearly all women — would drop on to her bent back. Sometimes, when the first boat was filled, an Arab would catch the pilgrim on his neck, and she could then be seen riding him away as a woman rides a bicycle. From one boat to another he would leap, with his helpless victim, and finally pitch her forward over his own head into an empty boat, where she would lie limp and helpless, and regret it some more.

I saw one poor girl, with great heavy boots on her feet, with hobnails in the heels, fall into the bottom of a boat; and before she could get up, three large women were dropped into her lap. Just then the boat, being full, pulled off, and I saw her faint, and her head fall back; and her death-like face showed how she had suffered. It was rare sport for the Moham-medans.

"Jump!" they would say to the Christians. "Don't be afraid; Christ will save you!"

It was 4 P. M. when the last of these miserable people, who ought to have been at home hoe-ing potatoes, left the ship. An hour later, a long dark line of smoke was stretching out across the plain of Sharon, behind a locomotive

drawing a train of stock cars. These cars held
the seven hundred pilgrims bound for Jerusalem. It will be midnight when they arrive at
the Holy City, and they will have no money
and no place to sleep in. Ah, I forgot ; they
will go to the Russian Hospice, where they will
find free board and lodging. It is kind and
thoughtful in the Russian Church people to
care for these poor pilgrims, now that they are
here ; but it is not right nor kind to encourage
them to come. It will be strangely interesting to them at first ; but when they have
seen it all, there will be nothing for them but
idleness ; nothing to do but walk, walk, — up
the Valley of Jehosaphat, and down the road
to Bethlehem.

Jaffa to Jerusalem

———•———

JAFFA was the home of Simon the Tanner, whose house still stands, and is now for rent. It was the shipping station of Jonas; the port where Solomon landed the cedars of Lebanon, with which he built his extravagant harem; and out of the wreck-strewn reef that frowns in front of the custom-house, rises the rock of Andromeda. It was here the poor lady was chained; but it was not the sea monster she feared, but a change in the wind. If the wind had blown from shore, and brought to her the faintest whiff of Jaffa, she could not have lived to tell her tale. When you land here, — which you can accomplish only when the sea is calm, — you find yourself in a narrow, mean, muddy street, filled with freighted camels, *hamals*, and burres, through which you are marched for a quarter of a mile before you come to a road wide enough to hold a carriage ; then you look across the street, see Howard's Hotel, dismiss the carriage for which you have paid a tourist agency a dollar, and walk to your stopping place.

We landed at 10.30, and by 10.45 we had become tired of the sights and scent of the city. Securing a guide, I waited upon the chief of the Jaffa and Jerusalem Railway.

It was Saturday; the manager — whom I could not see — said he was very busy, but if I would come in to-morrow, he would be glad to give me any information I desired. I went straight to the station, caught the 12.15 express, and entered the only first-class carriage in the train, with a ticket for Jerusalem. The road is a three-foot gauge, the cars are narrow, and only half of one little pine coach is set apart for first-class passengers. This space is cut by a partition making two boxes, six by seven feet, for tourists.

The train is made up of all kinds of cars. The grass is green between the ties, and the scale that is crumbling from the sandstone cornice of the station is allowed to remain

where it falls, to be crushed under the feet
of the travellers. The management is French,
with a strong Turkish flavor. The pompous, almost military-looking manager, and the brightly
uniformed "chef de gare," or station-master,
seem strangely out of place, when you glance at
the wretchedness that surrounds them. Here
is a queer mixture of the frivolity of France
with the filth of the Orient. From the time
you get the first glimpse of the Jaffa *gare* till
you reach Jerusalem, the whole show has about
it an air of neglect like a widow's farm. They
appear to know as much about railroading as
the average Arab knows about the Young Men's
Christian Association.

The time was up, and we were fifteen minutes
over-due to leave, when I asked Howard, the
hotel man, what the matter was.

"Waiting for *le directeur de la compagnie*,"
said he, with a smile; for he knew how absurd
it was to hold the only daily train the road runs
for the General Manager.

Another quarter of an hour went by, and still
another.

Suddenly there was a bustling among the

station-hands, the bell jingled, the whistle — the deep-voiced North American Baldwin whistle — sounded, and we moved away. At the last moment I saw the handsome station-master hurry a well-dressed gentleman to our car, put him in, and then swing gracefully into the second-class carriage immediately behind ours. A couple of officers of an English war-ship which was anchored off Jaffa occupied one of the first-class compartments, and now the new-comer came in where I was.

The train started slowly, and seemed to be running over a track made of short pieces of rails; but I soon found that the one wheel at my corner had three flat spots on it, and that the two rear wheels had but one. This gave the car an uncertain sort of movement, two short hops and a long one. I looked at my companion and tried to look pleased. He frowned. I raised the window and tried to see what made the car caper about so, and my travelling companion burnt a cigarette.

"Little rough," I said as a feeler; and my friend blew such a fog into my face that I was obliged to take to the window again.

" Window too cool for you? " I asked, venturing another flyer at the Frenchman, and he scowled.

Growing accustomed to the pounding and bucking of the carriage, I began to look at the strange scenes along the line. On one side there was an orange orchard, whose trees were laden with golden fruit. On the other was an olive orchard, and here and there tall date-palms flung their banners to the breeze. In a field near by, a native was ploughing with two little thin-legged blond cows, followed by another team which was a strange combination, — a burro and a bull; and just behind that a tall camel came swimming slowly through the peaceful air, drawing a wooden plough which had but one handle. This is a beautiful valley, called the Plain of Sharon; and if it was farmed as France or England is farmed, it would be a veritable garden. Forty-five minutes out we stopped at Lydda, twenty kilometres from Jaffa. Here my friend got out, walked up towards the engine, scowled, and returned to the car. The red-fezzed station-master from Jaffa came from his carriage, just as the station-master of Lydda came out of the station. Their eyes met ; they stopped, clasped their hands, and you could see in a minute that they belonged to the same lodge. The Lyddian tilted his head slightly, as a hen does when she sees a hawk high above her ; then they *unplaited* their fingers, and rushed into each other's arms. When they had embraced, the chef from Jaffa held the Lyddian off at arm's length, and looked calmly into his eyes, as if to say : " Hast thou been faithful to thy trust ? Lie not ; for behold the breath of the high chef des gares is upon thee and will wither thee if thou speakest not the truth."

The Lyddian nodded his head three times very slowly, and the chef kissed him on the right and then on the left cheek. Another deep blast from the Philadelphia whistle, and my carriage began to scamper away like a wounded hare in the stubble. Another quarter of an hour brought us to Ramleh — old Arimathæa. One hour from Jaffa, and this Syrian cyclone, this Jerusalem jerk-water, has covered nearly eighteen miles. I dropped off as the train was coming in, and made a picture of the pretty little station. Ramleh is an old town, — in fact, everything is old here. The railway, which was opened only two years ago, is old, and only a few people came to see the train go by. It has always been a place of importance, for here the old caravan road from Damascus to Egypt crosses the trail trod by the Crusaders from Jaffa to Jerusalem. At Lydda I fancied I smelt a hot-box; then I laughed at the idea, — a hot-box at eighteen miles an hour! It was only the odor of the Orient, I reasoned, and forgot. But now, as the train stopped at Ramleh, two clouds of beautiful blue smoke came up from a coal car near the locomotive, and floated away across the rolling plain. The doctor of the battle-ship and his friend the lieutenant were contemplating one of these boxes, when I came up and offered to bet a B. & S. that my side would blaze first.

"Taken!" said the game doctor; and while we were amusing ourselves thus, my French friend came forward, saw the hot-box, and made a bee-line for the station.

The next moment he was out again with the conductor. You could see that the box was not the only thing hot on the J. & J. The distinguished traveller was beating his hands

together, pushing his nose sideways with his
front finger, and telling the conductor things
that would burn the paper if we printed them.
When he stopped to breathe, the station-master
of Ramleh, — who had already been hugged
and kissed by the station-master from Jaffa, —
pulled the bell, and the train started. My travelling companion then turned on the poor
station-master for having started the train while
he was busy roasting the conductor. He raised
both hands above his head and rolled off a
succotash of French and Arabic for a whole
minute ; and when he turned, the rear end of
the train was just disappearing over a little hill
beyond the switch, and the General Manager
— *le directeur de la compagnie* — was left
behind.

I believe he must have been glad of it, for
he knew enough English to know that English
officers were making jokes of his railroad, and
that I was not over-pleased with the flat wheels.

The land was still beautiful. A little way
to the south was the broad valley of Ajalon,
where Pharaoh conquered a king, and gave
the ranch to Solomon, together with his

daughter; for it was plain to Pharaoh that Solomon was wasting a fortune trying to create a boom on Mount Moriah, which is in Jerusalem, —the only place where they suffer from drought and mosquitos at the same time.

"Sun, stand thou still on Gibeon, and thou, moon, in the valley of Ajalon. And the sun stood still, and the moon stayed, and there was no day like that before it or after it." So it is written of the valley of Ajalon; and now the sound of a locomotive whistle floats o'er the plain, and echoes in the hills of Judæa.

"I win!" said the Doctor, presently, pulling his head in from the open window. "Mine's burning beautifully."

Leaving the plain, we enter a cañon about six hundred feet above the sea, up which we toil at a snail's pace. The country grows more desolate, the hills are barren wastes of gray rock, with not enough vegetation to pasture a tarantula. When we had arrived at Beir Aban, thirty-one miles out, time two hours and fifteen minutes, and the station-master from Jaffa had embraced and kissed the station-master at Beir Aban, first on the right cheek, and then on the left, the cloud of smoke that arose from the two hot boxes hid the locomotive entirely. For a half-hour the train crew carried water from the tank and flooded the hot boxes. The same was repeated at Bittir, — even to the kissing and embracing, — and we were off on the home stretch for Jerusalem, which is twenty-six hundred feet above the Mediterranean. The cañon grows narrower as we ascend, and still there is no earth in sight, — nothing but rock, rock, everywhere. Sometimes we can see on the sides of the terraced hills a few rows of olive-trees, which, like the scrub cedars in the mountains of America, seem to spring from the very stones.

The conductor — the slouchy, careless, polite conductor — came through the car for the last time, and every one was glad we were nearing the Holy City. The train-men are all French, and, like most French people one is compelled to rub up against in the churches, theatres, and shops of the Republic, — especially in Paris, — they appear never to use water, except the little they put in their claret. There are more fountains than bath-tubs in Paris. French people in the lower walks of life remind one of the Mohammedan making a pilgrimage to Mecca, who obstinately refuses to bathe until he gets there, — only these people seem never to get there ! There 's the sea at Jaffa; but these fellows never think of using it, any more than the natives do.

The conductor is in keeping, however, with other things pertaining to the road. Their "cabinets de toilet," supposed to be built for the use of the public, are absolutely unapproachable. They are as far below those of France in the way of cleanliness as the latter are below those found in England. I have never seen such inexcusable filthiness in any country. Even the Arabs notice it.

The distance from Jaffa to Jerusalem, according to Howard's "Guide to Palestine," is thirty-two miles as the raven makes it, and thirty-six by wagon-road. No guide-book has been perpetrated since the opening of the railway; but none is necessary, as the time is about the same. In fact, "White Sheik" — Howard's Arabian steed — beats the train as often as he is ridden down from Jerusalem.

The distance by rail is eighty-seven kilometres (about fifty-four miles), according to
the time-card ; and the same makes the running
time four hours and ten minutes : but we lost
an hour to-day.

The fare, first-class, is $3.00, second-class
$2.00, and third-class $1.25. The road has
never earned operating expenses, I am told,
and never will, I am led to believe. The locomotives are the best mountain locomotives
made ; and that is about the only thing they
have to speak of.

I think there must be something in the
Brotherhood of Station-Masters prohibiting the
sweeping of floors in stations, as they are all
covered with sand, dirt, and scraps of paper,
and things.

I travelled over a little lumber road in Texas
once, whose initials were T. & S., and the train-
men called it the " Trouble and Sorrow," and
sometimes " Timber and Sand." I rode on
the locomotive, for it was the first wood-burner
I had ever seen. The train was carded at
twelve miles an hour, and we were losing time ;
but it was the only time I was ever frightened

on an engine. The road was so rough, and the engine rolled so, that the hazel-splitter hogs would scamper out of the ditches beside the track. In places the track was so sunken that the ties hung to the underside of the rail; and when the engine struck a place like that, and drove the ties down, the mud and water would shoot out over the face of the earth, and fresco everything inside the right of way. The passengers, if they had not been too frightened, could have picked flowers from the windows of the rolling coaches — almost. Till now, the T. & S. has been to me the rockiest road on earth; but now — it's all changed.

Now the whistle sounds deep and long, the train has reached the top of the cañon, the end of the gulch, and here before us, nestled in the very top of a group of little mountains, is Jerusalem. The sun is just going down in the hills through which we came, and away to the east, beyond the Dead Sea, the hills of Moab are taking on the wonderful tints they wear at sunset. They are unlike any other mountains, in that the crest-line is as straight as the line of the horizon on a level plain.

How strange it all seems ! There is nothing but rocks, and scrubby olive-trees, and dead-looking grape-vines, — and not many of them. The people are strange, too. On the way to the hotel, we pass all kinds of people of the Orient, — Bedouins on high horses, with their knees cocked up; plains-men on thin-legged Arabian steeds; all manner of men on donkeys and on foot, — beggars, and even lepers, and poor Jews; Jews with cork-screw curls hanging down in front of their ears, and idle pilgrims who do nothing on earth but walk, walk up the valley of Jehosaphat and down the road to Bethlehem.

The moment you have seen it all, Jerusalem becomes to you the most melancholy locality on the face of the earth. It was so with us, I know; and when the time came to leave, not one of our party missed the train.

When the Syrian cyclone begins to descend from Mount Zion to the sea, you are led to believe that you will reach Jaffa in about an hour; but when the train has gone a quarter of a mile the careful driver reverses the engine, opens the cylinder-cocks, and you think by the

swish, swish, of the escaping steam that there is
an open switch just ahead ; but you are always
wrong. The truth is, they have no air-brakes,
and the driver is obliged to hold the train with
the engine in the back-motion until it is brought
down to a reasonable pace. When you have
nearly stopped you go ahead again, just as you
did before, and go on repeating the perform-
ance to the bottom of the hill, twenty-five miles,
and two thousand feet below Jerusalem. The
balance of the journey over the Plain of Sharon
is less hazardous. The engine-driver is a
Frenchman, and extremely careful and compe-
tent. He never allowed the train to get beyond
his control for a single moment, and he has, on
the whole, about as difficult a run as there is
east of Pike's Peak.

At Jaffa, as at Constantinople, you must take
to the sea again, for there are no more railroads
here.

After the Jaffa and Jerusalem, the P. and I.
is good to look upon. This little railway
runs from Port Saïd to Ismaïlia, less than a
hundred miles. The gauge is not even three
feet, — which seems to be a sort of standard

for narrow-gauged railways everywhere. It is
only thirty inches. The locomotives are like
toy engines, but good ones, and the carriages
are beautiful, — perfect little palaces. ø They
are not only neatly designed and artistically
constructed, but scrupulously clean and very
comfortable. They are narrow, of course, but
ample room is given to each passenger. They
are so arranged that the whole car may be
opened up, allowing one to pass through it
from end to end. I had no time to inform
myself regarding the road's history, but I was
told that it had been built and was being operated by a French company. I hope so, for
the J. & J. has rather disgraced France. The
rail, which rests on metallic cross-ties, looks to
be about thirty pounds to the yard. The road
runs, for the greater part, along the Suez Canal,
with the sea on the other side; and the ride
from Port Saïd, if the sand is not blowing, is an
interesting one.

In the shallow sea to the right are myriads of
sea-birds of every conceivable kind, and farther
out, hundreds of sleepy-looking little ships with
one sail, whose masts lean back like a slender

palm in a steady wind. To the left is the
canal, upon whose narrow waters one sees the
flag of almost every civilized country, save perhaps the Stars and Stripes, which, somehow,
one seldom sees at the Orient, — or anywhere
else, for that matter. Even at Constantinople
the flag at the embassy flies only on high days
and holidays, — and not very high then.

With all their enterprise, this company make
one serious mistake. They refuse to " paste "
baggage through from Port Saïd to Cairo, and
at Ismaïlia the traveller must hunt out his luggage, and have it re-weighed and re-registered.
The P. & O.'s beautiful new steamer Caledonia,
bound for India, had unloaded an English
excursion party the day I went down, and it
took nearly two hours that night to re-weigh the
baggage where we left the smart little railway
and boarded the Egyptian line.

The Egyptian state railways are not bad, nor
very good, but they answer the purpose. Their
locomotives are fair, their cars are of the usual
European style, short and light. They make
very good time, too, for such a slow country;
but one must travel first-class always in Egypt,

to avoid smoke, filth, and dirt of every kind, — the quick and the dead !

If the reader has ever ridden on the rear-end of an American railroad train, and is of an observing turn, he has noticed that the moment the train passes a gang of section-men, they all fall to as vigorously as though they were repairing a wash-out, and were holding the President's special. "Poor fellows," says the sympathetic traveller, "how they work!" He does not observe that every Irish son of them has one eye on the track, and the other on the rear-car looking for the roadmaster. Well, they do that here, and the Arabs did it on the Jaffa and Jerusalem, — just as the Chinamen do in California, and the negroes in Texas. Human nature is much the same the world over.

Relations of the Employee to the Railroad

12

RELATIONS OF THE EMPLOYEE TO THE RAILROAD

———•———

AS the shifting sands in the bed of a river are constantly changing the channel, so are the conditions of the country constantly changing the relations of the railroad employee to the railroad.

When the country is prosperous, and all the railroads are running full-handed, employees are apt to air their grievances and ask for a raise in wages as often as a dividend is declared. When times are hard and hundreds of idle men are abroad in the land, and locomotives are rusting in the round-houses, railway managers are apt-to ask the employees to submit to a reduction in wages as often as a fresh batch of men are discharged and sent adrift. These facts may not be very complimentary to either side, but they are facts, I fancy, all the same.

The railroad company proper is regarded by the average employee as a mythical soulless something, ever invisible and always out of reach. The struggle is really between the men and the management, — the employees and the officials; and as they are all employees, — from the president to the tie-tamper; from the master-mechanic to the poorly-paid wiper, — we must have a division to begin with. Out of this great body we must find the fighting forces for two armies, absurdly arrayed, one under the flag of " Capital," the other bearing the banner of " Labor."

This condition of things is all the more inconsistent when we remember that the real fighters are all laborers; only, one side has succeeded, the other is struggling to succeed. And how are we to know them? When does the " employee " become an official? Ah, that 's the easiest thing in the world. For example, this change in the life of a locomotive-engineer comes the day he is promoted to be travelling engineer or round-house foreman. It comes to the conductor when he is made superintendent of a division; to the telegrapher when he

becomes a despatcher or train-master. The
other employees come in awkwardly, congratu-
late the new official, and then go back to the
boarding-house and lock their trunks. Here is
a parting of ways. From this day the new
official walks on the other side of the street,
regarding the promotion (for which all are striv-
ing) almost a misfortune. At the end of a
week his room-mate leaves him, and he goes
also, — to live in a better place. At the end
of a fortnight he finds that he has, almost un-
consciously, changed his mode of living and
his associates.

He sits no longer in the councils of employees, for he stands for the company, — for
Capital. In many cases he pays up his dues
and takes an honorary membership, or with-
draws finally from the Brotherhood. He is so
different in his new place that sometimes he is
accused of being " stuck on himself." I put it
that way, for it is precisely as the " other fellows " will put it; and I have dwelt upon this
point to show that there is no mistaking an employee for the " company," which is simply the
management. It would not be just to say that

the new-made officer deserves all the bad things said of him, nor would it be right to say that the unpromoted employees are wholly to blame. They have simply all dropped down the wrong leg of the " Y," and nobody has taken the trouble to back them up and set them right. Then it is always so much easier to convince a working-man that he is getting the worst of it than to show him that he is prosperous and ought to be happy. That's why the professional agitator has such smooth sailing. Man is a scrappy animal at best, and I think that the constant strain under which the railroad employee works tends to make him especially irritable, as the constant watchfulness of his nature tends to make him suspicious of signals which are not perfectly plain to him.

The railroad manager at his office, dictating letters, directing business, and hearing grievances, is a different man altogether when seen at the club, at the races, in Sunday-school, or at home ; but the less-experienced employee is always the same on and off duty. He has not yet learned how to forget his work, to put it aside, and rest his weary brain. He railroads, not only earnestly, but all the time : on the rail, in the round-house, the barber-shop, and the boarding-house. When he wants his plate changed, he tells the waiter to " switch out the empty, and throw in a load."

The little jealousies and animosities just described exist among the employees as well as between the man and the managers. For years the bitterest hatred existed between the Brotherhood of Locomotive Engineers and the Brotherhood of Locomotive Firemen. Until lately a member of the latter organization was not eligible to membership in the former. In the West, where promotion comes quick and easy, where the fireman of to-day is the engineer of to-morrow, where the world seems wider and ideas broaden, these narrow views found little favor. Indeed, it was the Western delegates in the convention who caused these restrictions to be removed.

There existed for years the bitterest hatred between the members of the Order of Railway Conductors and the Engineers' Brotherhood. So cordially did they hate each other that it was almost impossible to get good service.

Railway managers made no frantic effort to bring about a reconciliation between these important branches of the train service. On the contrary, I am afraid some of them rejoiced in the strife, knowing well that so long as labor warred with labor, capital would have smooth sailing.

When the Knights of Labor were in their glory, many railroad employees turned to that organization as the coming Moses. This led up to a struggle between the Knights and the Brotherhoods.

When Debs — often wrong, but always honest and earnest, I believe — conceived the idea of bringing all railroad employees together in one colossal Brotherhood, he found himself opposed by all the older organizations, including the Brotherhood of Locomotive Firemen, for whose advancement he had spent the best years of his life. Just as the different nations of the earth train their cannons on the other shore, so do the various labor organizations of the United States "lay" for one another.

Happily, thoughtful men are beginning to regard all this as quite unnecessary, as a great waste of energy; and a change is coming. Looking back over the fields where labor and capital have fought, we see only waste, want, desolation, and death. In struggles of this kind capital gains nothing, and the best labor can get is the worst of it. The great strikes of the past twenty years, including the last bitter struggle of 1894, must prove plainly to the thoughtful working-man that he must rely mainly upon his own ability to make a place for himself in the world and to hold it.

The struggle between the American Railway Union and Mr. Pullman in the beginning, the railway companies of the country in the end, has proven two facts: to capital, that it is just as well to treat fairly and deal honestly with labor; to labor, that the country is not ready for anarchy. Few people believe that the acts of lawlessness committed at Chicago were the doings of working-men. These outrages were committed mainly by idle loafers and criminals of every cast and from every country. Foreign working-men, at best, appear to bring all their grievances, all their disrespect for law, — in short, all they possess that is un-American, —

to America. In nearly all the labor disturbances the finger-marks of the foreigner are plainly visible. The long and lawless struggle at Cripple Creek was organized and officered wholly by foreigners, and their energies were directed mainly against one American, — self-made as far as his fortune is concerned, — who, in the panicky winter of 1893–4, advanced nearly $100,000 to build a railroad to the great gold camp, thereby providing work for hundreds of men who were actually hungry. I find no fault with a man because he is a foreigner ; only, if he cares to live in the United States, he ought to respect the laws of the country. But when an American journal, or news-gathering association, will interview an Anarchist upon the murder of the president of a republic, allowing him to rejoice in cold type over the death of a distinguished citizen of another country ; then, when Americans allow such a man (a murderer at heart) to live in the land, Uncle Sam becomes an accessory, and by his tolerance encourages Anarchy.

I have seen their emblems. Here, in Paris, not more than a mile from where I write, there is a corner in the graveyard set apart for these miserable people. The walls are all ablaze with red rings, a sort of bloody funeral harness, and on their shields, red with rust, are engraved the knife, the pistol, and the torch. It is not good for the young republic of France, with a new-made grave of a murdered president, to allow these things to hang here, with their breath of danger and hints of death.

It is not difficult for one, even slightly acquainted with the history of the railroads of the United States, to pick out those that have been most prosperous; and it is gratifying to note that those roads enjoying the greatest prosperity are generally at peace with their employees.

We have seen the unpleasant side of the employee, — how, in the past, peace seemed to trouble his mind, — and now we shall see the other side.

He is not only capable of appreciating humane treatment, but is as loyal to the company employing him, when properly handled, as the highest officer can possibly be. Cross him, and he will fight for his manager. Ask his opinion, and he will show you how far the

"Thunder-bird" of his line is ahead of the wretched and rickety old "Night-hawk" run by the opposition road. The enthusiasm of the earnest and industrious passenger-agent and his army of assistants seems to find its way down the line to the humblest employee.

I don't pretend to say that such is always the case. A great deal — nearly everything, in fact — depends upon the character of the higher officials. A railway manager, the fingers of whose 'phone run down to the pool-rooms and the gilded palaces of painted women, will have a demoralizing influence upon the employees of the road. Turning restlessly in his office-chair, ever gazing out at the window to fields which he fancies elysium, ever impatient and anxious to get away from work, to return to play, he cuts everything short, and you will find his subordinates following in his footsteps.

Take the manager who is thoroughly in earnest, honest and loyal to the company, and his influence will be felt. It is not difficult for a manager to win and hold the respect of the employees of a railway. If he but takes the trouble, and has the happy faculty of imparting

a little human kindness to every employee with
whom he comes in contact, he will soon win
the respect of all his subordinates. In doing
this he makes his own labors lighter, and at the
same time adds to the happiness of the employees and the revenue of the road. The
best service can be had only when all work har-
moniously and with a will. Railway employees
know when they are treated decently. They
know, too, that an impartial judge, commonly
known as " public opinion," will pass upon
their cause, and they are learning rapidly that
it is not good to kick unless they have a " kick
comin'," as they express it. The best of them
are not great readers, but they manage to
acquire more knowledge of things in general,
and railroads in particular, than the average cit-
izen does. Go and mingle with a band of yard-
men who are loafing round a switch-engine, and
in a half hour you will get a good bit of the history of American railroads, and much of the
personal history of the leading railway officials
of the country. You will find, too, that, if they
" roast " some of them vigorously, they praise
others enthusiastically. It is always pleasant to

say nice things of other people.   It is pleasant
to try to pick out the good things in the life of
a man whom the public has regarded as bad.
Jay Gould, for example.   The employees of
railroads commonly known as the "Gould
Systems" were always sure of three things,
— good wages, decent treatment, and a good
check for their money the moment they earned
it.   This respectful consideration for his employees, which was one of the noble traits in
Mr. Gould's character, has been imparted to
his assistants, and is distinguishable to this day.
Not long ago, during an inquiry by the Government into the matter of wages of employees,
the president of one of these roads was called
to the stand to testify.   When the venerable
railroader took his place and raised his hand to
be sworn, his white hair falling like a halo about
his head, the United States judge looked at
him for a moment, and said : "You need n't
swear."   Perhaps the judge remembered that
in that same city — then a wild outpost of civilization on the Western plains — this man
had begun his railroad career as a humble
employee, and that in all these years his

honesty had never been questioned, and that was sufficient.

Perhaps it was not much to take his testimony without swearing him, but to me it seems a delicate and touching compliment to this great good man. I know it is customary to preserve these little flowers for the grave, but I prefer to put this one here. It may serve as a "marker" to those who follow in his footsteps, — a something to strive for, "a consummation devoutly to be wished."

I never knew Tom Potter, never saw him, but I know he lived and died. I remember that for a year after his death it was impossible to open one of the many trade magazines, printed and supported by railway employees, without reading a line like this: "Send something to the Potter Monument Fund." I do not know that he ever got the monument, but I know he got its equivalent, — a monument of devotion which can only be built on the foundation prepared for it in life. It proves that in the average railroad employee there is a pay-streak of gratitude; and that ought to make up for a multitude of short-comings. But it is not

necessary to die in order to receive his respect.
During the hard times in the West, caused
mainly by the closing of the silver mines, a
very conscientious general manager called a
number of employees together to discuss the
matter of a reduction of wages. There were
present representatives from the various brotherhoods and labor organizations who had been
sent to head-quarters instructed to submit to
no reduction of wages. The manager made his
case so clear — showing the delegates the utter
impossibility of keeping all the trains then on
the time-card running, and the folly of sup-
posing that the owners of the road would retain
him as manager unless he made some effort to
reduce operating expenses to fit in a measure
the decrease and still decreasing earnings —
that he at once won the respect of the dele-
gation. When these poor fellows returned to
their several homes and made the result of
their deliberations known, there was a great
row. Some of the more ignorant and unscru-
pulous employees openly accused the delegates
of selling their constituency to the railroad.
The manager heard all this in due time, and,

having faith in the justice of his cause and the humanity of man, he submitted the question to a vote of all employees, with the promise that wages should be restored at the beginning of the following year. The men voted to submit to the proposed reduction ; but few of them ever knew what want and misery they saved by so doing, for, if the manager had been beaten, the force was to have been reduced, and thus many of them would have been thrown out of work entirely at the beginning of a hard winter, when all the railroads in the country were discharging men.

A less thoughtful, a less humane manager, would have ordered the reduction in wages which circumstances certainly made necessary, and created a strike, — won in the end, at the expense both of the employees and of the stockholders. It is well to observe these things and the way they work. They all show that a straightforward, open, and honest policy will often save money for the people who have been enterprising enough to build railroads, and prevent the less-learned employees — the fretful children of the rail — from running blindly into danger.

13

I happened to be in San Francisco when Mr. Stanford died, and I want to say a word for him. If you ask me how he managed to save twenty millions in twenty years, I cannot answer; but there was something good and gentle in his nature. Poor Mr. Stanford! Surrounded as he was with his miserable millions, with all his wretched riches, his going away was as peaceful and pathetic as the death of a nun. He knew, it seems, that he was going, and had selected his pall-bearers. They were the six oldest locomotive-engineers in the employ of the company. Many times he had placed his life in their hands, and now at the end he wanted these strong, brave fellows to " handle his train " on the last sad run. As usual, they did their work well, walking upright with a firm step. Their eyes were tearless, their faces calm; but if you looked closely, you would see them trying to swallow something. It was that hurt in the throat that comes to men — unfortunate men — who are not weak enough to weep.

At the other end of the procession another band of employees walked, with bowed heads and tear-wet eyes, — yellow men, whose homes and gods were at the other end of the earth, who found the paths at the Occident slippery ways; but they had taken something of the tenderness of their gentle master, and so walked in his wake and wept.

From the Cornfield to the Cab

EVERY boy, arrived at a certain age, wishes to take part in the work of the world which he sees going on about him. Many desire to become locomotive-engineers, but few of these understand how hard and long is the way to gratification of that ambition. My experience is like the experience of many a man who has worked his way from the corn-field to the cab of a locomotive.

My first railroading was in the humble capacity of a water-carrier for the graders on the Vandalia road, in Illinois, where my father had a small contract. Finally, the grade was completed, and the construction train came along behind the first locomotive I had ever seen.

Of course I was deeply impressed with its grandeur. Every boy gazes at a locomotive with rapture, partly compounded of fear. If boys playing football hear the whistle of an engine, they will stop and look. A boy swimming, who is supposed to forget everything, will turn and swim on his back and watch the train go by.

Our farm lay near the railroad, just at the end of a hard pull. From the field where I worked during my youthful years I could see the fireman at his furnace, while the great black steed toiled slowly up the hill with a half a mile of cars behind her. I never looked with envy at the engineer. If I could be a fireman, I thought, my cup of happiness would be full.

It is not an easy matter, without influential friends, to get employment on a railroad, especially if the applicant happens to have hayseed in his hair, or milk on his shoes. When the brakeman, who is the paid elocutionist of the train crew, wishes to humiliate a fellow-workman, he invariably calls him a farmer. No greater insult can be offered to a brakeman.

I had lived a quarter of a century, and failed in half a dozen business ventures, when I decided to go railroading, being prepared to accept the humblest position, so long as it was in the path that led to the throttle.

I presented some strong letters to the Master Mechanic of the Denver and Rio Grande at Salida, Colorado; a clerk wrote my name and address in a large book, saying that he would call me when I was wanted. I began to think I should not be wanted; for I had waited a month or more when the caller came one evening and told me to report to the night foreman.

First I joined the wipers, — a gang of half a dozen men, whose business it is to clean the engines up when they come in from the road. This gang is made up of three classes, — old men who are not strong enough to perform heavier work; young and delicate youths; strong young men who expect to become firemen when their names are reached.

The wiper's work is not arduous, except for the long and dreary hours, — from six in the evening to six in the morning. But it is disagreeable work. You have to get down in the pit under the locomotive reeking with oil, and wipe the machinery clean and dry with bunches of waste. All this time you are obliged to inhale the awful fumes of the torch you carry.

If you are faithful and patient, you may be promoted to the day shift in six months. Here you perform the same work, but without the torch, and you sleep of nights. By and by you are promoted again to the position of engine watchman.

There are from twenty to fifty locomotives in the round-house, and it is the watchman's duty to keep water in the boilers, and enough steam up to move the engines in case one is wanted in a hurry. Before long the foreman, if he thinks you deserve to be encouraged, will put you on a yard-engine as fireman. This will take you back to night-work, but it is one step forward, and the work is light.

When there is a vacancy you will be given a day engine, and again you feel thankful: you see the sunlight; it gives you courage; you are glad to be free of night-work. I do not know of anything that will embitter a man's life and sour his disposition so swiftly and surely as working week after week through the hours of darkness.

From the day yard-engine you go out on the road, and now you are a real fireman. You are assigned a regular locomotive, and you are expected to keep everything clean and in order ; that is, everything above the running-board, — that board which you will see on all locomotives, extending from the cab along the side of the boiler to the front end.

On mountain roads, ten years ago, wipers, watchmen, and all round-house helpers were paid one dollar and seventy-five cents a day, firemen on yard-engines two dollars, and engineers three. Firemen on road engines received two dollars and forty cents a day, and engineers four dollars ; but Eastern roads do not pay nearly so well. I know of a half-dozen railroad presidents who began at less than fifty cents a day.

Another great advantage the men of the West had at that time was that they served, as a rule, less than three years as firemen, though now on Eastern roads men commonly fire from five to ten years. But the West was then developing rapidly, and new roads were being built every year.

At the end, say, of three years, the fireman may be promoted to be hostler. The hostler takes the engines from the coal-track, side-track, or wherever the engineers leave them. He has them coaled up, the fire cleaned, and then runs them into the stalls in the round-house. In this work he becomes familiar with each and every engine on the division, and if he be observing, he will retain this knowledge and use it when he becomes an engineer.

The next promotion takes the hostler back to the night yard-engine : this time as engineer. His pay is now three dollars a day, or ninety dollars a month ; but he was making over a hundred dollars a month at two dollars and forty cents a day as fireman.

Road engine-men are paid by the mile, — forty-four mountain miles or eighty-five valley miles being a day's work. Thus, when business is good, the engine crew make forty and fifty, and once in a while sixty, days in a month.

The man on the night yard-engine goes through the same stages of promotion that the fireman went through, until at last he finds himself at the throttle of a road engine, with another increase in pay and a corresponding increase in responsibility, but with less real hard work to perform.

On some roads a man must, I believe, serve a time in the shops as helper and machinist before he can hope to be promoted to the position of engineer. This is not absolutely necessary, for the reason that the engineer is not required to keep the engine in repair. Most master mechanics will tell you that the machinist is not always the best " runner."

There is a book called the work-book, where the engineer whose engine needs repair writes its number, what he wants done, and his name. If he is not quite sure about the disease, he may make a report like this : " Examine right steam-chest." The foreman will set a machinist to work, who, nine times out of ten, will locate the trouble in a very short time.

Even where promotion comes rapidly, it takes from four to six years to work from the wiping gang to the cab ; but these years are not wasted. Every day and every hour you become more and more acquainted with the various parts of the great iron horse, till at last the knowledge picked up in these years of toil serves to make up the sum of your education as a locomotive engineer. The years seem surprisingly short, for there is always the hope that springs eternal to lure you on.

The life of an engineer is fascinating, especially where the road lies along the banks of a beautiful stream, or over grand mountains. Here at every curve a new picture is spread before him.

To reach the summit of some high mountain at sunrise; to look down the winding trail which he must travel, and see the blue-jay cloud lying across the track; to dash through the cloud and out into the glad sunlight again, the verdant valley stretching away below, — the high hills lifting their hoary crests above, — is apt to impress one with the awful grandeur of God's world, so that he will carry that impression through life.

A very small percentage of locomotive-engineers become railway officials. If promotion comes to the engineer, he is usually promoted to the office of travelling engineer. The duty of this officer is to go about over the road to see that the engines are made to work to their full capacity, and to see that the engine-men do not abuse the engines or waste the supplies.

The travelling engineer usually recommends firemen for promotion. While railway rules permit the promotion of firemen in accordance with the length of time they have served in that capacity, the rule is not always applied; and it should not be. One man will learn as much in a year as another will in ten, and all men do not make good engineers. Then, again, if a man is given to dissipation, he is not, and should not, be promoted in his turn.

There is a vast improvement from year to year in railway employees as a class, morally and intellectually. It is no longer considered necessary for a man to be "real tough" to be a good train or engine man. As a class, the men who now enter the railway service are more intelligent than those who sought such employment fifteen or twenty years ago.

The travelling engineer is often promoted to the position of master mechanic; from that place to superintendent of motive power; and sometimes he becomes superintendent of the road, or general manager.

Among the boys who read this, there may be some who desire to become locomotive-engineers. To such I would offer one bit of advice, —do whatever you are assigned to do cheerfully; and do it well.

Never leave a piece of work half done. Try to be the best wiper in the gang; the best fireman on the road; but do not say you are so. The officials will find it out, if you are really deserving of recognition.

Do not rely upon a grievance committee to hold your job; take care of that yourself. Remember that it is easy to "kick" yourself out of a good place, but never into a better one. The official who promotes you is in a measure responsible for you; see that he does not have to apologize to his superior for your failure.

The moment you become dissatisfied with your position, quit. Think it over first, and see whether you can better your condition; but do not drag others into your troubles; learn to rely upon yourself.

If you succeed in reaching the right-hand side of a locomotive, you will then be in a position to show your fellow-workmen that a man may be a smooth runner without the excessive use of tobacco, liquor, or profanity.

By pursuing this course, you may be regarded as a curiosity by some of the fraternity, but you will be respected by the men and the management, you will live longer, and you will be happier while you live.

14

Rhymes of the Rail

To the General Passenger Agents

I dedicate these simple lays
To the jolly, joyous G. P. A.'s
Of America, whose " paper-talk "
Has saved me many a weary walk.

CY WARMAN.

●

THE FLIGHT OF THE FLYER

NEAR where the hill-girt Hudson lay,
　　Up the steel track the engineer
Reined his swift steed at close of day,
　　As, leaping like a frightened deer,
At each wild surge she seemed to say :
Away ! Away ! Away ! Away !

The slow team toiling up the hill,
　　The light boat drifting with the breeze,
The swiftest trains seemed standing still ;
　　Red vines were twining round the trees,
Whose leaves, made golden by the frost,
Gained more of lustre than they lost.

The trackman, tamping up the rail,
　　Felt the perfume of dying flowers ;
The shadows lengthened in the vale,
　　And watchmen watched from out the towers
The little cloud of dust behind,
As we went whistling down the wind.

Night's curtain falls; and here and there
   The housewife lights the evening lamp;
And where the fields are cold and bare,
   His fire is kindled by the tramp.
Down throught the midnight, dark and deep,
The world goes by us, fast asleep.

Up through the morning, on and on!
   The red sun, rising from the sea,
As we go quivering through the dawn,
   Lights up the earth, reveals to me
In the first ruddy flush of morn,
The golden pumpkins in the corn.

From east to west, from shore to shore,
   The black steed trembles through the night,
And with a mighty rush and roar
   Breaks through the dawn; and in their flight,
Wild birds, bewildered by the train,
Dash dead against the window pane.

" Be swift," I cried, " oh, matchless steed;
   The world is watching, do your best!"
With quick and ever-quickening speed,
   The hot fire burning in her breast,
With flowing mane and proud neck bent,
She laughed across the continent.

FROM BUDAPEST TO BELGRADE

BOUND for the Orient, I strayed
　　Down by the Danube near Belgrade,
The Servian capital.
　　　　　　　　I had,
For guide that day, a Servian lad,
A rider; but you'd never guess
He rode the Orient Express
　　From Budapest to Belgrade, then,
　　From Belgrade back to Buda 'gain.

He had the softest, sunny hair!
　　His eyes were like the Danube, blue;
And, looking on him, one would swear
　　Whatever tale he told was true.
So young and fair, you'd never guess
He rode the Orient Express
　　From Budapest to Belgrade, then,
　　From Belgrade back to Buda 'gain.

His story was not new to me,
  For strange things happen on the rail,
  And we have heard a wilder tale,
Of sea-men rising from the sea
  Who had been dead a week, whom men
  Had not a hope to see again.

"See there, where treads the watchman's trail,"
  Said he. "One night, as I came down,
  Just while I whistled for the town,
The head-light shimmered o'er the rail
  And showed a woman running there
Like some wild wingless bird of night,
And, rippling o'er her robe of white,
  A sable cataract of hair :
  I thought a ghost was running there.

"She turned — I saw her — 'God, Clairette !'
  I gasped, reversed and set the air,
  With naught of time nor space to spare.
I saw her death-white face, and let
  The sand fall, threw the throttle wide,
  And cried, O Heaven ! how I cried
                              To her.
"We stopped ; I saw her fall
  Beneath the wheels. And when she fell

I sprang to rescue her, and — well —
She disappeared ; I tried to call
                                To her.
" Three times I called her name
And listened ; but no answer came,
    Although I stood just where she fell.

" Remembering that her father's cot,
    Beyond the bridge, was near the track,
I turned, and hurried toward the spot,
    And saw the river running black
Just where I stopped and trembled on
The brink, for lo, the bridge was gone !

" The Angel slept ; but love had found
    A way to warn me in her sleep,
    God bless her.
                        At another bound
    I must have gone down in the deep
Dark Danube ; in that awful flood
Whose mere remembrance chills my blood."

   .   .   .   .

The same man rides the night express ;
    The self same man who rode it then,
Rides twice a week to Budapest,
    From Budapest to Belgrade, then,
    From Belgrade back to Buda 'gain.

AT THE ENGINEER'S GRAVE

HOW often, at night, when I 'm rocked o'er
    the rail,
  When the little stars shine overhead,
My mind wanders back over memory's trail,
  And I think of the days that are dead.
The red locomotives we had for our toys,
    The coaches so gaudy and gay,
How we played together, Bill, when we were
      boys,
    And again I can hear you say:
" Chu-chu, chu-chu, here comes the railroad,
  " You 'll be the brakeman and open the bars."
Big bell a-ringing, somebody singing,
  " Chu-chu, chu-chu, here come the cars."

And now, where your sleep is so dreamless and
    still,
  In this silent city I stroll;
Oh, send me some signal, or speak to me, Bill;
  How is it, old friend, with the soul?

How is it up there on your heavenly railroad?
  The moon for a headlight, for white lights
      the stars ;
  Glad bells a-ringing, angels a-singing,
  " Chu-chu, chu-chu, here come the cars."

THE FREIGHT TRAIN

HOW I love to watch the local winding up
    around the hill,
In the sunrise of the morning, when the autumn
    air is still,
And the smoke, like loosened tresses, floats away
    above her back,
And to listen to the measured *Choo-ka, Choo-ka,*
    of the stack.

The man who rides these mountains, whose
    fiery steed of steel
Drinks of Nature's flowing fountains, must inev-
    itably feel.
A divine and peerless painter spread the scenes
    along the track
As he listens to the *Choo-ka, Choo-ka, Choo-ka,*
    of the stack.

In the peaceful hush of midnight, when his
    pilot ploughs the gloom,
From a hundred hills wild-roses send their subtle
    sweet perfume
To the wary, weary watcher, whose lamps light
    up the track,
And a hundred hills give back the *Choo-ka,
Choo-ka*, of the stack.

Ah, how I miss the music of the whistle and
    the bell,
And the breathing of the air-pump, more than
    any tongue can tell;
And the mighty, massive Mogul seems to try to
    call me back,
With her *Choo-ka, Choo-ka, Choo-ka, Choo-ka,
Choo-ka* of the stack.

CHIPETA[1]

WHEN *Uncompahgre's* vale I view,
  From mountains high and hoary,
I seem to dream love's dream anew,
  And hear the old, old story.
Chipeta, blest queen of my breast,
  When here mine eyes first saw you,
The *Poncho* perfumed wind caressed
  Your sun-kissed *Wahatoya*.

O'er *Alamosa* hills we strolled,
  Whose shadows seemed to beg us
Pause where gentle *Lomas* rolled,
  Above the Verdi *Vegas*.
The soft wind shook the *Arboles*,
  And song-birds in *La Jara*
Make music dulce on the breeze
  From *Elko* to *Cuchara*.

[1] Italics are names of stations on the Denver and
Rio Grande Railway.

Oft in these *Cimarron* ranges grand,
    The walks of *Escalante*,
Have I caressed your sun-browned hand
    With kisses *Caliente*.
Dear, good Alcalde, bring her back ;
    No monte is *Bonita*,
O'er whose rough *Piedras* there's no track
    Made by my lost *Chipeta*.

Or take me to Thee, *Manitou*,
    My *Santa Fé* will guide me,
And some day I shall be with you,
    And walk with her beside me
Upon that blest *Hermosa* shore,
    So sunny and *florida*,
Mine anima shall mourn no more, —
    I see the soul's *Salida*.

OUR HEROES

WHEN we have scattered the flowers of May
    Over the graves of the Blue and Gray, —
Over the graves where the women weep,
Over the mounds where the heroes sleep, —
Then let us turn to the graves of those
Who have lived and died in their over-clothes.

Are they not heroes? have they not died
Under their engines, side by side?
Have they not stood at the throttle and brake,
And gone down to death for their passengers'
    sake?
Calm, undisturbed, be the peaceful repose
Of the men who have died in their over-clothes.

I would not take from the soldier's grave
Not even the blades of grass that wave;
Nor do I ask you to hand me down
A single star from the soldier's crown;

All honor to him : but forget not those
Who have lived and died in their over-clothes.

'T would be sweet to know, when they're laid
    to rest,
With hands folded silently over their breast,
That a woman would come to their graves once
    a year,
Bringing wreaths of flowers ; that a woman's tear
Would dampen the dust on the graves of those
Who have lived and died in their over-clothes.

15

THE TRAMP'S LAST RIDE

THE brakeman pulled his double-breasted
   vest, and threw himself astride
The brake-wheel; then he said he guessed as
   how the road warn't justified
      In totin' people on their gall
      Who had no travellin' card at all.

Then to the sunset, far away, the poor tramp
   looked with tearful eyes;
He viewed the distant dying day, turned to the
   shack with some surprise:
      "'Then you won't tote me?" "No," he
         said;
      "I 'll never tote you, 'less you 're dead."

The tramp was bound to have a ride; and from
   his torn and tattered coat
A flask of Leadville-suicide he pulled, and tipped
   it down his throat;
      Then, to the brakeman turned, and said:
      "Git ready, pard, I 'll soon be dead."

THE NELLIE BLY

A MAIDEN to Chicago bound,
  Cried, " Bissell, do not tarry,
And I 'll give thee a golden crown
  To fly me o'er the prairie ! "
" And who be ye this trip would try,
  And who 's his jags, the flunkey ? "
" Oh, I 'm the girdler, Nellie Bly,
  And this, my Indian monkey."

" Then look well to thy wardrobe, lass,
  There 'll be some lightning changes
From California's field of grass
  To Raton's rocky ranges ;
From Glorietta's polished peaks
  To th' warm Arkansas valley,
We 'll do in days what once took weeks."
  " I understand," said Nellie.

Then o'er the track the special sped,
  And o'er the wire the warning ;
The mile-posts from her pathway fled,
  Like dew-drops in the morning ;

Across the hill and down the dell,
    Past station after station,
The muffled music of the bell
    Gave voice to each vibration.

Swift speeds the steed of steel and steam;
    And where the road lies level,
The train sweeps like a running stream,
    Past palace and past hovel.
And o'er the prairie, cold and gray,
    There falls a flood of fire,
While orders flash for miles away:
    "Take siding for the Flyer."

The engine seems to fairly float,
    Her iron sinews quiver,
While swift, beneath her throbbing throat,
    The rails rush like a river.
Upon the seat the engineer,
    Who knows her speed and power,
Sits silently without a fear,
    At sixty miles an hour.

NOBODY KNOWS

NOBODY knows when the song-birds sing,
    In the first glad flush of the summer sun,
The want and the woe that time will bring,
    When the season has changed, when the
      summer is done ;
When the flowers and ferns sleep under the
    snows,
    What will the winter bring, nobody knows.

Nobody knows, when we say " good-by "
    To our wives and our babies, and hurry away
O'er the glistening rail, 'neath a sunny sky,
    How we 'll return at the close of the day,
Hearty and hale, or shall we repose
    Cold in a casket : nobody knows.

THE OPEN SWITCH

A LL the summer, early and late,
    And in the autumn drear,
A maiden stood at the orchard gate
    And waved at the engineer.
He liked to look at her face so fair,
    And her homely country dress ;
She liked to look at the man up there
    At the front of the fast express.

There 's only a flash of the maiden's eye,
    As the engine rocks and reels ;
And then she hears in the distance die
    The clinkety-clink of wheels.
Clinkety-clink, so far apart
    That nothing she can hear,
Save the clink of her happy heart
    To the heart of the engineer.

Over the river and down the dell,
    Beside the running stream,
She hears the sound of the engine-bell,
    And the whistle's madd'ning scream.

Clinkety-clink; there's an open switch, —
  Kind angels, hide her eyes!
Clinkety-clink: they're in the ditch,
  Oh, hear the moans and cries!

Clinkety-clink, and down the track
  The train will dash to-day;
But what are the ribbons of white and black
  The engine wears away?
Clinkety-clink! Oh, worlds apart,
  The fireman hangs his head;
There is no clink in the maiden's heart:
  The engineer is dead.

THE ORIENT EXPRESS

A BOLD Bulgarian shepherd-boy, who looked
    so like a sheep,
  So gentle, yet so sportive in his showy shep-
    herd's dress,
Lay down upon the railroad track and played he
    was asleep,
  To fool the engine-driver on the Orient Ex-
    press.

The driver, who disdained to slay the ram upon
    the rail,
  Put on the brakes, reversed the wheels, and
    turned his face away.
The stoker stood beside him, for it seemed his
    heart would fail,
  Whereat the shepherd-boy stood up, and
    laughed, and ran away.

Then came the Irish section Boss, the day the
    train came back,
  And poured about a barrel o' tar between the
    ties that day ;

So, when the shepherd-boy lay down, the tar
  upon the track
  Trick'd through the whiskers of his robe,
  and held him where he lay.

The driver could not hear the cry that swept the
  right of way, —
  The death-cry of the shepherd, — and his
  soul was filled with mirth.
He opened up the throttle-valve, and turned his
  face away :
  The train bore down upon the boy, and swept
  him from 'he earth.

THE FELLOWS UP AHEAD

FORTY miles an hour when you're sailing
    through the air,
When you read the daily papers in a soft reclin-
    ing-chair;
Forty miles an hour when you slumber in your
    bed:
Do you ever give a thought to the poor fellows
    up ahead?

When the road is rough and saggy, and the
    snow, and sleet, and rain
Falls, and freezes on the headlight, while their
    eager eyes they strain
Just to catch a little glimmer of the trail the
    wheels must tread,
While the storm beats on the faces of the fellows
    up ahead;

When the lightning leaps and flashes through
    the spires and splintered crags,

And the engine shrieks and dashes o'er the hills
and through the sags,
When in secret with your conscience, your evening prayers you 've said, —
Make a little requisition for the fellows up
ahead.

AN OLD STORY

THIS morning I read an old story, —
    I 'd read it before, long ago ;
'T was one of those painfully hoary,
    But touching old chestnuts, you know.

I knew when I read the first stanza,
    When the " mad train was dashing along,"
And the passengers " peered from the windows,"
    I knew then that something was wrong.

When the mile-posts, a million a minute,
    Were flitting and fluttering by,
I knew that our poet was in it,
    I knew he was going to lie.

When the stoker said, " Stay at your post, Jack,"
    And the sun sank away in the west ;
When "a grim face appeared on the pilot,"
    I anticipated the rest.

Then the glad mother rolled in the rag-weeds,
  "Me boy, oh, me baby!" she cried,
And the train went away in the twilight, —
  And the creative poet had lied.

DEAD

" DEAD ! my queen," said the engineer,
      And something stole silently over his
      face,
And left in its travels the trace of a tear.
" Dead ! " he said, bending over her bier ;
   " Dead ! and the world is an empty place.

" Only this morning she bounded away,
   Radiant, beautiful, tossing the snow,
Brushing the drifts from her path away ;
It seemed so selfish in me to stay,
   And slumber and say that I could n't go.

" Dead ! and oh, such a little while
   Ago so bright ; " and he bowed his head,
And his face wore a sort of a bitter smile,
As he leaned o'er the wreck in the old scrap
      pile
      And murmured : " My little McQueen is
      dead ! "

THE COUNTRY EDITOR

THE dear good country editor sits in his
dingy den,
And writes of needed railroad laws for the ben-
efit of men
Who owe six years' subscription to his patent
inside sheet,
Who shun the starving scribbler when they see
him on the street;

Who sing their psalms in Sunday-school with
accent soft as silk,
Who mingle saw-dust with their bran, and water
with their milk;
"What time's the 2.10 train depart," the editor inquires,
Remembering that on New Year's eve his annual
expires.

He dons his silken bell-top tile, and takes him
to the town;
He tints the city for a while, and then he
journeys down

Among the great monopolies whose slaves op-
  press the poor,
And with a gall immaculate he pauses at the
  door.

His faith now seems to falter, there 's moisture
  in his eye ;
But with a conscience ballasted with the Rock
  that 's in the Rye,
He enters and announces, as chipper as a lass,
" I 'm Boils, the Blue Creek Blubber man, —
  just please renew my pass."

STANDING HIS HAND

A STEER stood on the railroad track,
 Whence all but him had fled ;
The flames from out the engine stack
 Shone round his curly head.

Yet beautiful and bright he stood,
 And held the right of way, —
A beast of royal Durham blood,
 A terra-cotta bay.

" Ring off, ring off," the driver cried,
 " You offspring of a gun ; "
And but the bounding wheels replied,
 And fast the train rolled on.

The train rolled on, — he would not go
 And join the common herd ;
The farmer heard the steam-cars blow,
 The while the steer demurred.

15

Then came the train at sixty miles.
The steer, oh, where 's he gone?
Ask of the section boss, who smiles,
And sips his beef bouillon.

THE OLD ENGINEER

WHEN years after years are gone and for-
    gotten ;
When soft silvery ringlets your temples adorn,
And fall round your forehead like fragments of
    cotton ;
When the last breath of youth's scented sum-
    mer is gone, —

Keep this unpretentious poetic epistle ;
    'T will bring back the mem'ry of days that
        were dear ;
Think of me kindly, then, list for my whistle,
    And say, " 'T is my friend the old engineer."

WHEN YOU ARE GONE

To S. T. S.

HOW strange the place will seem
  When you are gone;
When, doubting my ability to hide
  My sincere sorrow, gazing on
The face of your successor, I shall chide
  Me for the little good I 've done, —
  When you are gone.

Think not that I engage
  Your manly mind
With worthless words and idle flattery;
  I 'd only have you know you leave behind
A faithful friend, whose swerveless constancy,
  Esteem and loyalty live on
  When you are gone.

LOCH IVANHOE

UP near the mountain's craggy crest,
  The mighty moguls, strong and proud, —
The snow-drifts beating 'gainst their breast, —
  With pointed pilots pierce the cloud.
High mountains, seeming little hills,
  Emboss the spreading plain below,
And rivers look like laughing rills
  As down the distant vale they flow.

Here in a weird cold wintry grave,
  Wrapped in a marble shroud of snow,
With not a ripple, not a wave,
  Calmly sleeps Loch Ivanhoe.
But with the coming of the spring
  The little flowers will bud and blow,
And gladsome songs the birds will sing
  Along the banks of Ivanhoe.

www.ingramcontent.com/pod-product-compliance
Lightning Source LLC
Chambersburg PA
CBHW030759020726
47499CB00006B/1691